HARD
TO BEAR

A Bear Jacobs Mystery

Linda B. Myers

About This Book

Hard to Bear is a work of fiction. Names, characters, places and happenings are from the author's imagination. Any resemblance to actual persons – living or dead – events, or locales is entirely coincidental.

No part of this book may be used without written permission, except in the case of brief quotations in critical articles and reviews. Email inquiries to myerslindab@gmail.com

Published 2017 by Mycomm One

© 2015 by Linda B. Myers

ISBN: 978-0-9986747-2-8

Book Design by IntroStudio.me

For updates, news, blog and chatter:

www.LindaBMyers.com

Facebook.com/lindabmyers.author

www.amazon.com/author.lindabmyers

myerslindab@gmail.com

Dedication

For my sister, Donna Whichello.

Bear doesn't have a clue without her help.

PROLOGUE

Pain.

As Solana Capella came to, she groaned, her head pounding like a jack-hammer.

What happened to my head? Ouch, my arm. Where ...?

Her eyes fluttered open and slowly focused on the feral eyes of a swamp monster staring back. Pain was joined by its old friend, fear.

But wait. Not a swamp thing.

The hollow-cheeked face wasn't really green. It was smeared with camouflage muck. The stranger was pushed up against her and seemed to be spreading the same green and brown ooze on her face.

Panic.

She yelped and began biting and scratching at Camo Man's hands. She inhaled the breath she needed for a championship scream, but his enormous hand clamped down over her mouth and pinched her nose, shutting down the air passages. She fought, but he tightened the grip. "Shhh," he hissed low as a whisper. "They're coming. You must be very still. Do you understand?"

They're coming? Oh, God.

Now she remembered. She tried to control her fear of this new captor. She did her best to nod and, failing at that, blinked her eyes rapidly. Maybe he'd take that as, "Yes, I understand." He may hurt her, but at least he wasn't one of them.

Any old port in the storm, right?

She felt a hysterical bubble of laughter behind the hand over her mouth as it eased up, letting air rush into her lungs. He glowered a warning at her, then slithered down prone, pressing hard against her. That shoved her backside up to a damp cold wall of earth. The kind with spiders and centipedes and worms. She shivered, pressing back against him in hopes of moving her ass off the wall.

Solana was afraid she would suffocate as her face squashed into his slender chest. But some deep instinct of a small cornered animal told her to be ever so quiet, to freeze in place. Playing dead, she took inventory. From the little she could see pressed against him, it appeared they were in a shallow, low cave. Roots from a million plants laced through the dirt and clay, holding its walls in place. It smelled of mold and rotten vegetation, overcoming even the fetid odor of filthy clothes and man sweat crushed against her nose. She could hear the sound of rushing water, and through the mouth of the cave, she was aware of only deep grey light. It must be nearly dark.

The pain reasserted itself. They had not marked her body. The scrapes, bruises and sprained wrist were from her wild flight. The real ache was buried deep within, raw and torn, from the rape. She shuddered against this stranger who now held her fate in his control.

Fear had been her companion since she'd been taken. It rose and fell like swells on the ocean. Now it was ebbing, as she accepted that Camo Man was helping her hide from them. When she felt his muscles tense, hers followed in lock step. Then she heard the sounds he was hearing.

Movement in the underbrush above. More than one hunter. Footsteps overhead, coming to a halt. Shuffling feet. Men swearing.

Flashlight beams crisscrossed the grayness in front of the cavern's opening. Then she heard in a voice she knew, "It's too dark. We'll miss her again. She'll be easier to track in the morning. Killing this bitch will be more fun than most."

They left. It was still. A minute, five, maybe a year. Then the man next to her moved back just enough for her to see his face. "They call me Ghost," he said. "You knocked yourself out trying to run under a tree limb. I brought you here. But we have to move on."

She considered his ragged military jacket as well as the face paint. "Are you a soldier?" she whispered.

"Was. Can you walk?"

She nodded, although she was unsure how far she could go. Her stolen sandals were no more than shreds now, one sole flapping loose against the bottom of her foot. She'd run so far, so fast that vine maple whips and blackberry thorns had cut her feet and her legs. The cowboy shirt she'd taken was so big it had caught on snags, and now shreds flapped like home made fringe. Same with the basketball shorts. But she was a fighter, and she would not give up. Her sister's life depended on it.

Ghost turned and slid on his butt out of the cave. "Follow," he said and she did, mimicking his action. As she slid out and down, he caught her just as her feet entered the freezing water of a fast moving creek. She gasped.

"We'll walk in the creek for a while. No tracks to follow. No detectable odors unless they bring dogs tomorrow." Ghost headed upstream.

Solana looked back at the cave but could not see the mouth. It was hidden in the dusk behind the grasses on the bank. Her instinct was to go back there and hide forever. But she told herself it would not be so hard to see in the daylight. She had to swallow her exhaustion and fear.

Her baggy shorts rode so low on her hips that they dragged in the water. Holding them up with one hand, she followed Ghost. He seemed to sense where he was as the darkness became absolute, the journey only lit in patches where pale blue moonlight soaked through the forest canopy. He grabbed her uninjured wrist to lead her, and in time the freezing water dulled the pain in her feet. It seemed like a thousand miles until he stopped and pointed up the bank.

"There," he said. The massive root system of an ancient Sitka spruce looked like clutching fingers in the moonlight. The tree must have crashed to earth many decades before. Now other trees were growing from the nurse log which was at least twelve feet across near the base. The massive old roots swept out into an impenetrable arch of tendrils that intertwined with boulders rising above the muddy bank.

Ghost left the creek and pulled her up the bank to the far side of the roots where they jammed against a casket-sized chunk of volcanic rock. "Kneel here and crawl forward."

She did as she was told. On her knees she could see that there was room for her to shimmy between two tangled roots. She crawled through and found herself in a hollowed out cavern inside the fallen tree.

Ghost followed her in. He reached for a flashlight tucked inside the entrance and turned it on. "This is one of my hidey holes," he said to her. "Nobody knows it. We're safe. For now."

Solana watched him open the padlock of a battered foot locker with a key that hung on the chain with his dog tags. He lifted the lid of the locker and handed the flashlight to her. "You can leave it on for a little bit."

While he removed fur pelts from the locker and spread them over the bottom of the cavern, Solana flashed the light around her. She could see the space was a circle with maybe an eight foot diameter. "How did you do this?" She asked. "It's awesome."

"Burned it. Like some tribes hollowed out trees to make canoes." Next he rummaged out several strips of jerky. "Venison," he said, handing some of the dark, smoky slices to her. "Eat then sleep. We'll leave at daylight."

Solana took two of the pelts and crawled under them. If he meant her any harm, there was little she could do about it. She tried to chew the tough meat, but she was so tired. Too tired. The last thing she remembered was Ghost pulling out a satellite phone and calling somebody named Vinny. They made plans to meet. Solana was asleep before she heard where or when.

CHAPTER ONE

Case Notes
September 16, 2 p.m.

Society places certain expectations on Italians like Frankie Sapien-
za. Maybe his family puts horse heads in each other's beds. Maybe
they use car trunks as portable caskets. A person can be forgiven for
thoughts like these if you've seen enough movies.
The rest of us residents at Latin's Ranch Adult Family Home are
fascinated with the Sicilian octogenarian. After all, gossip is our nu-
mero uno group activity. We like to speculate that he's a don of the
highest order. But, alas, Frankie pretty much keeps his trap shut no
matter how much the rest of us bump our gums. Oh, he's a smoothy
all right, with a fine line of patter when it serves his purpose. But
about his past he reveals zip, zilch, nada. And we don't push it, not
as long as Frankie's goomba Vinny Tononi hangs around looking
threatening as a hawk in a henhouse.
Maybe my roommate Eunice Taylor could make some inroads now
that she's what Frankie calls his little dove, which is apparently
somewhere between first date and betrothed. But she doesn't ask him
awkward questions. She likes him and the gifts he bestows, but she
isn't actually interested in sleeping with any fishes. Eunice is smart
that way.
Anyhoo, imagine my surprise when Frankie up and asked Bear Ja-
cobs to handle a private investigation. That's right. The could-be

capo, who should have a lot of young hot shots on his payroll, chose
a cane wielding, overweight, grouch of a has-been shamus to trust. I
take it as a show of respect for Bear's brain. Bear takes it as nothing
less than his due.
Of course, when he elicited Bear's help, the secretive Sicilian didn't
mention that the rest of us would soon be hiding a terrified young
woman. Or that murderers might climb right over us to get to her.

- Lily Gilbert, Curious Assistant to PI Bear Jacobs

Lily Gilbert shut down her laptop, sat up and swung her leg over the side of the bed. Ever since she had become the eWatson to retired private investigator Bear Jacobs she'd kept her version of case notes. They weren't official files, of course, in the sense of admissible court documents. There were no "pursuant tos" or "time of the incidents." But they were the kind of notes that appealed to Lily, and if Bear needed something else, he could go find another assistant who worked for goose eggs. He could do that right after he pounded sand.

She fluffed up her cloud of light gray hair, pinched a little more pink into her cheeks, and hopped down from the bed on her one remaining foot. With the help of her walker she traveled out to the Latin's Ranch kitchen in search of a cup of tea. Lily actually knew that Bear was grateful for her case notes and even more so for her help. But everyone had been a little edgy since Frankie had consulted with Bear. What the hell was up?

Bear Jacobs, Lily Gilbert, Eunice Taylor and Charlie Barker had all come to the adult family home together, after departing a nursing home. Frankie Sapienza was the only resident who had arrived from points unknown. Latin's Ranch was a lot smaller, friendlier, and homier than a nursing home. And usually safer, too, from things like communicable illness.

But safer from gangland warfare? Well, that wasn't the kind of thing most care facilities worried about. It hadn't been an issue at Latin's Ranch either until Bear gathered the other residents together to tell them what Frankie wanted him to do.

"He's honorable by crook standards," Bear had begun. "His family made their living in the traditional rackets of gambling, protection and prostitution."

Eunice's feathers ruffled. "A friendly card game or two, maybe helping a few storekeepers out with security, but prostitutes? Not my Frankie." Her lips compressed into a tight little pout as she crossed her arms over her kaftan-covered chest. With that orange spiky hair she looked like an irritated pin cushion.

Bear rolled his beady black eyes. "Right. Not that. What was I thinking?" He crossed his own arms over a chest covered by an ancient flannel shirt that must have been an XXL.

Lily the Peacemaker quickly intervened. "Keep going, Bear. I'm sure there's more you want to tell us."

"Okay, but only if you're interested," Bear grumped.

Lily knew the big man could pout every bit as well as Eunice. Based on his mass, Alvin Jacobs might have been a retired lumberjack instead of a sleuth. He was in his seventies with silvertip hair and beard surrounding his massive head. Size and hair together provided his nickname. But Lily knew that *Bear* described his personality, too. He could fool you into thinking he was a big ambling dope, slow and easy to underestimate. You'd be wrong. Bear was steely sharp. It was never wise to underestimate him.

"We're all interested, Bear," Charlie said, glancing up from the hand of solitaire spread on the living room game table. He was tall enough that his voice should be in the basso profundo range, but instead, it was sort of a squeak. "Really. Tell us."

"Okay. As I was saying, the Sapienza family made its nut in traditional cri- , um, pursuits. Frankie has his standards." He tipped a metaphorical hat to Eunice.

She brightened and returned the nod vigorously, moussed spikes bobbing with her. "Thank you, Bear. Of course he does."

"He says he never condoned things like street drugs or kiddie porn or the slave trade. All the seamy shit that newer gangs are into. To an old Italian like Frankie, *newer* gangs mean Latin or Asian or Russian." Bear paused, momentarily pushing out his lower lip before saying, "And, to be honest, I've never heard about anything like that in Frankie's past."

Bear should know, Lily thought. He'd had a long career as a private investigator before bad health ended it. If the cops had dirt on Frankie Sapienza, he'd have heard about it. As far as she could tell, Bear's noggin was a bulging filing cabinet of all his past adventures.

"Frankie's heard rumors of a business one of those gangs has started. Innocent people dying in a bizarre way. In his system of ethics, it's bound to bring the wrong kind of attention to mob activity, and that's bad. He wants it stopped. He doesn't want organized crime under a spotlight. I imagine none of the families really want one going rogue."

"Why did Frankie come to you with this, Bear?" Lily asked.

"You think I'm not capable?"

"Oh, quit it." Lily took just so much guff from her old friend. "You know I mean instead of going to one of his own people."

"He wants to know exactly what's happening, and which gang is behind it. He can hardly go to the cops. And someone in his own family would be recognized by the others." Bear leaned forward in his easy chair and looked from one to the next. "I'm telling you about it because you all have a decision to make."

Our ears cocked like bird dogs sighting quail.

"A frightened girl was found out in the woods by one of Vinny's pals. She's involved in this somehow. Thugs were chasing her and are still trying to hunt her down. She needs a place to hide until I can hear her story and work this all out. A place nobody would guess."

"A place like Latin's Ranch?" Charlie piped up.

Bear nodded. "You guys willing to hide her here? Could be dangerous."

Invite murderers into our little safety zone just to help a girl we don't know?

Even as she thought it, Lily said, "Of course."

"Of course," said Charlie still slapping red cards on black.

"Of course," said Eunice, giving Bear a why-would-you-even-ask shrug.

Bear nodded at his little band of operatives. "Good thing we all see eye to eye. Because she'll be here tomorrow."

"But Bear, you need to ask Jessica about this first," Lily cautioned. Jessica Winslow was the owner and caretaker of Latin's Ranch as well as Lily's closest friend. Jessica believed the seniors in her care needed a certain amount of freedom and control over their own lives, that being old didn't make them a bunch of big babies. But would she allow them to put each other in danger?

Fat chance.

"No, Lily," Bear said. "We'll get the girl here first, then *you'll* tell Jessica."

"Me?"

"Sure. That's what BFFs are for."

CHAPTER TWO

Case Notes
September 16, 4 p.m.

The girl arrives tomorrow. Frankie told Bear she was found in the woods by a former special ops buddy of his bodyguard, Vinny Tononi. Just being Vinny's pal makes him one spooky dude in my book. It really ups the stakes when you know the guy's name. It's Ghost. Yeah, normal people walk around with a name like that. Ghost.
After a lunch of our cook's homemade enchiladas – with the best kick ass salsa in todo el mundo – Bear and I figured out what to do with the girl when she arrives. First, we considered the layout of Latin's Ranch. It's a rambling affair that was a farmhouse at the beginning of its life. After Jessica decided to take us in, the upstairs was expanded and a wing was added with a porch across the front and a patio across the back. A lot of it was done with my daughter Sylvia's money. More about her later. She's on my list of worries, too.
Anyhoo, Jessica lives here along with the five of us residents, plus Ben Stassen's daughter, Rachael, and her baby. Ben is Jessica's hunka hunka but he's not a live-in, at least not yet. We also house a fat cat, a dog with a limp and two canaries. The staff includes two aides, Aurora the cook, and a youngster who swing-shifts as Aurora's kitchen slave and housekeeper.
It's a full house. There's certainly no room to hide another person. Outdoors, there are the sheds, riding ring, and horse barn. Fertile

pastures are surrounded by woods, a mix of deciduous trees, cedar and fir typical of the Pacific Northwest. It's all owned by Jessica who splits her time between caring for us and caring for horses. She boards them for other people, gives riding lessons, and raises a breed called Paso Finos. The Latin's Ranch name came from her stallion, Latin Lover.

"There's only one place on this property that Jessica doesn't feel free to go uninvited," I said to Bear. There was little chance Jess would agree to this plan, and until we sprang it on her, we needed a place to hide the girl even from her.

Bear was ahead of me. "Sam's trailer."

Sam Hart is Jessica's barn manager and handyman. He lives in an old Airstream between our house and the barn. "Bingo. But we can hardly put a girl in there until we get Sam out."

"I imagine he would notice a thing like that."

We sat on the patio in the sun. The days are still long enough for a breezy warm afternoon. It makes me think of my garden, the one that was sold along with my house when I went into the nursing home. I loved that garden, even the autumn chores that coaxed it into glorious bloom the following spring. But I've come to love Latin's Ranch about as much. In some ways maybe even more. Proof that there's at least some gold in the golden years.

"We could talk Sam into taking a vacation. Frankie would probably pay for one."

I was pretty sure Bear knew that was hopeless when he said it. "He wouldn't leave the horses with no notice to Jessica." Sam loves those hay burners almost as much as she does. If horses can have bodyguards, they have one in Sam.

We sat and rocked and thought and rocked. Bear hummed Come Fly with Me. He always hums old standards while he thinks.

"I've got it," Bear said. "The dogs."

It took me a sec before I caught on. "Yes, of course!"

Other than Folly, the cocker/dachshund mix that Jessica calls her cockadock, pooches are canis non-grata around the ranch these days. A pack of feral dogs had attacked her colt, Latin Dancer. They had *severely damaged him in the flesh and in the spirit. He would never make a show horse or command a stud fee as high as his sire. It was a heartbreaking loss to Jessica's emotions and financial plans, even though her lover, Ben Stassen, bought the colt. Jess trained Dancer for him, and Ben will use him as a trail horse.*

The night it happened, Sam shot one of the dogs, a Rottweiler. It was tearing off a piece of the colt's hide at the time. The rest of the pack took off unmolested. Nobody knows for sure if they were wild marauders or local dogs banded together for sport. Either way Animal Control hasn't been able to catch them, and that's a big worry for stock owners. Now, just lately, Sam has heard them again, howling in the night. They may be coming back around. His rifle sits next to his trailer door, loaded and ready.

"I think he'd move to the tack room in the barn to be closer to the horses," Bear said. "Leave the trailer for a few days. That's all it should take."

"He'll do it if you ask. But if Jessica probes for more of an explanation, he'll never lie to her," I said. And then I just had to add, "I won't either. I made a promise."

"Yeah, I know what you mean. After we get the girl here so Jessica can see it's really okay, we'll tell her."

"You mean the she-followed-me-home-can-I-keep-her defense?"

"Sure. Jessica would never turn down an animal in need. And old farts like you and me prove she's a marshmallow when it comes to people in need, too."

- Lily Gilbert, Needy Assistant to PI Bear Jacobs

The residents were in the living room, staring through the big front window at the long driveway. Lily figured they looked like meerkats with mobility equipment. Bear had asked Frankie to have the girl delivered in the afternoon because Jessica would be away at a Paso Fino show with her stallion, Latin Lover.

Lily agreed. "The timing is serendipitous."

"It's what?" asked Charlie. "Isn't Serendipitous that group from the sixties?"

"That was the Serendipity Singers, Charlie." Eunice focused a pair of mother-of-pearl opera glasses on the road which was barely visible at the end of the drive.

"Whatever. Nice young people. Those boys had short hair and ties. The girls wore skirts and curled their hair."

"Well, here comes Serendipitous now," Lily said, always eagle-eyed. They rushed outside as fast as a wheelchair, two walkers and a quad cane could rush. Only Eunice sailed along under her own power.

It was the first time any of them had ever seen Vinny Tononi's Cadillac look anything but sleek as a black panther. Now its hood was littered with twigs stuck in every crevice. Small fir branches clung to its mirrors, wipers and grill. The polish was scratched, and when Lily touched the hood, it felt sticky with tree sap. At least the car smelled fresh as a cedar chest.

Vinny Tononi was a hulking big guy who preferred dark glasses and darker suits. Lily maintained that if you really listened, you could hear his weaponry clank as he walked. With no more than a nod at the five oldsters and a baleful glance at the front of his car, he opened the Caddy's back door.

A waif stepped out and faced them. Little, fragile, with eyes that rivaled those old Keane paintings.

Lily thought she was one of the sweetest looking girls she'd ever seen. Seventeen or eighteen, maybe. Her slight build might make her look younger than she was, but the wounded look in her eyes aged her. Her brown hair hung straight to her shoulders as though it had been washed but not styled. She wore a new pair of jeans that were rolled at the ankle, and her blouse had fold marks. Even her athletic shoes were bright with newness. A bandage around her left wrist looked clean and newly applied.

As Vinny unloaded shopping bags from Fred Meyer, Lily moved forward. "Hello, my dear. We're so glad you are here. My name is Lily."

"This ez Solana," Vinny said, handing the shopping bags to the girl and going back to his stricken car. "She ez for your care now."

"This is Eunice, Charlie, Frankie and Bear. Once you're settled, Bear will want to speak with you. He's a private investigator. And a good one. Whatever is going on, he will fix it." Lily gave the girl an encouraging smile but received no such gesture in reply.

Bear bowed slightly, a nod of the head but not of the body. "We'll find the bastards, miss."

The girl eyed the old PI then backed away. Lily thought a frightened child might find his gruff manner intimidating.

"Please," whispered the girl looking back at Lily. "Can I talk with you instead?"

"Well, but - "

"That will work fine, Miss Capella. You tell Lily and Eunice your story," said Bear. "In the meantime, Vinny will take me to meet Ghost."

"Why didn't he come here?" Charlie asked.

Vinny, who'd been mourning over the hood of his car, said, "Ghost never talks with people. And even *more* never, does not leave the woods."

✦　✦　✦

Solana Capella didn't know whether to be charmed or scared shitless by these geriatric weirdoes. She was sitting next to Lily in an old trailer's tiny banquette, watching Eunice search from one cabinet to the next. "Lily believes in the restorative powers of tea. I myself believe the same about whisky. Ah! Here we go. Apparently, Sam Hart believes in both." Eunice assembled the ingredients, along with the honey and lemon she'd already found.

Lily looked at Solana and smiled before she spoke. "Sam vacated the premises earlier today. Set up a cot for himself in the barn's tack room. We're sure that will be okay with Jessica, our caregiver."

Solana noticed Eunice roll her eyes.

What's that about? Maybe I won't be staying here after all.

Lily looked calmer and smarter than the other one, maybe because she wasn't tinkling with jewelry and adrift on a sea of perfume. Too bad she only had the one leg. Solana wondered what it would be like, not being able to run.

Fucking scary, that's what.

She herself would be dead if she hadn't been able to race like a gazelle. Both old women were kind enough at least. Of course, Solana's experience with geezers was limited, but she knew they usually weren't scary. Maybe she'd be safe here until she could get to her sister. Surely the bastards wouldn't think to look for her in this place.

"You'll be snug as a bug until Bear can figure all this out," said Eunice as she fussed with the drinks. "You're just a child, but this much whiskey won't hurt you a bit. Warm you right up." She set the beverages down in front of them. One teacup had lost its handle and the others were mismatched mugs from Reggie's Tavern and the Black Sheep Diner. "The pickings are sparse in Sam's dinnerware department." Eunice seated herself on the other side of the table.

Meanwhile, Lily had booted up a laptop and looked ready to take notes, bony fingers poised above the keys. "Take your time now. And tell me what happened. But first, I guess we should call the authorities. Will you do that, Eunice?"

Eunice looked like a little kid told to go to her room. "I want to hear – "

"No," said Solana, sharply. "Nobody calls the authorities. It's too dangerous for Rosie."

It was the first thing she'd said since they came into the trailer. Lily and Eunice both stared at her. Solana looked from Lily's old face to Eunice's older one, making her decision. She needed to talk with somebody, and these two dinosaurs were all she had. Maybe it would be okay even if they were old. They didn't smell bad or anything, and a couple kids she knew actually liked their grams. She'd never met her own.

At least these two wrinklies are women. I'm sick of men. She thought about the ones she'd met outside, Frankie and Charlie and Bear. *Bear, right. How can that toothless old grizzly figure this out if I can't?*

She looked into Lily's clear eyes and saw the intelligence there. Slowly, awkwardly, she began to speak. "I don't trust the authorities for good reason. You know about homeless camps in the woods, don't you?"

"I know what I've read," Lily answered. "As the economy keeps tanking, many families reach the end of the line. They're living rough." She began to tap notes into the computer.

Solana nodded. "We lived with a family like that, my little sister Rosie and I. She's just fifteen. They were good people. Let us stay with them as long as they could pay the fee out at the county park." Solana glanced around Sam's comfortable but utilitarian mobile home. "This place is a palace compared to theirs."

"Sam's loaning it to you for as long as you need to hide."

Solana cringed with a shiver of fear. "Sam. He won't ... come for me, will he?"

"Sam?" Eunice and Lily asked looking surprised. "Sam would never hurt you," they continued in unison.

"He's a very good man," Eunice's earrings tinkled to punctuate her emphatic nod.

"I haven't met many good men," Solana said. "It's not been easy keeping Rosie away from pimps and sex slavers."

"No, I'm sure it hasn't," Lily concurred. Solana saw a warm shade of scarlet work its way up the old woman's neck and into her cheeks. "This country went to war against slavery over a hundred years ago. Now it's back, just in a different form. It's an outrage."

The old girl took a deep breath while her sidekick Eunice said, "The men you meet here have nothing but your safety in mind."

The men I've met here so far are too old to have anything else in mind.

Solana, slightly ashamed of that thought, continued. "The family we stayed with fed us and let us sleep in their pickup in return for cooking and cleaning. But the park kicked them out once they stayed the maximum amount of days. When they hit the road, they left Rosie and me behind. So we had to join eight other families living in the forest not far from the park. It's safer for us to band together. And when you stay near a park, it's not such a long walk to get to clean water."

"But ... but that's horrible for two young women," Eunice gasped.

"These camps are today's answer to the hobo jungles of the Depression," Lily said, one old hand leaving the keyboard to pat the hand of her friend. "Only instead of men on their own, these are families."

"Isn't it dangerous?" Eunice asked Solana.

"Duh," Solana said, instantly ashamed of her snotty tone. The old lady was probably just naïve, that's all. Most were. She softened her voice. "We only have tents and tarps, so we're pretty vulnerable to everything. Including each other. The camp managers, they're real careful about who they let stay."

"Can't you get help? Are you totally out of resources?" Lily asked.

"Where are your parents?" Eunice said at the same time.

Solana tightened her jaw to control her emotion. She'd learned tears rarely helped anything. But it had been such a long time since anyone had given a rat's ass about her. And now these old ladies acted really distressed. "For most people in the camp, public aid is long gone. Rosie won't go to children's services because she wants to stay with me. I'm her only family since we both had to get away from mom's boyfriend. I get some food stamps. And we go into town to look for work when we have the bus money. But that's a fuck-, um, joke. Even if we find jobs, nobody will rent to us without a deposit, and nobody at the camp has enough for that. So we're stuck."

"How long have you been there?" Eunice asked.

"Mmm. Maybe two months? The camp isn't supposed to be there, but unless someone complains, it's easier for rangers not to roust us. Or cops for that matter."

"Can you tell us about your kidnapping?" Lily asked, keyboarding away once again.

"The bastards are like invaders or something. Last time, they swept through screaming and knocking heads. This time it was a sneak attack. Either way, they take people away with them."

"You mean it's happened *before?*" Eunice took a big slug of her spiked tea.

"Twice that I know of. To an older guy and a boy about my age. But this is the first time they showed any interest in me." Solana's control abandoned her, and she began to weep. "What if they come for Rosie before I get back? And what will they do to her if I talk to the cops? I can't do that. And you can't either."

Lily leaned toward her. At first Solana stiffened, but then she allowed the old arms to close around her. They stayed that way for a long time, the girl expelling her fear and misery into the woman's circle of comfort.

Finally, Solana could continue. When she began again, the tale she told was like a horror story. Not just scary but brutal. Sick. It wasn't long before they all needed more whiskey, this time without the tea.

✦ ✦ ✦

Bear wasn't surprised when his roommate chose not to go with him to interview Ghost. Charlie had perpetual sores on his nuts from sitting in a wheelchair all day. The home care nurse who paid particular attention to that delicate situation was scheduled to visit Latin's Ranch late that afternoon. Charlie wouldn't miss the appointment for any amount of wealth or wishes.

Vinny drove the Caddy away from town and east toward Washington's Cascade Mountains. He left the highway on a two lane paved road that plunged into national forest land. It narrowed even more when Vinny maneuvered the huge vehicle onto a dirt track, punching a tunnel through cedar and fir. Bear presumed this had been a logging road many years ago. As branches slapped against the car, he understood why Vinny's prized possession was covered with twigs and pitch. He must have driven this way before when he picked up the girl, Solana.

Bear, in the backseat, listened when Vinny placed a call. "We are near," Bear heard him say. The dirt track petered out on the edge of a small meadow where there was just enough room for Vinny to turn the hulk around between volcanic boulders and enormous stumps from fallen giants.

"You okay, *Signore* Bear? We wait here."

Bear rolled down his window after Vinny shut off the Cadillac's powerful engine. It was impossibly quiet, as though every living forest thing knew humans as threatening interlopers. A breeze produced the only rustle through the leaves. Then, one brave bird began to sing again. Others joined until they harmonized in a merry racket. Bear never paid much attention to such things himself, but he knew Lily could have identified each singer, along with the wildflower remains that dotted the meadow. Now in September, the Indian paint brush, lupine and glacier lilies were brown or gone altogether, replaced by wild daisies. The breeze blew a chill through Bear's window. For a while he hummed *Autumn Leaves*.

Minutes passed without a word from Vinny. Finally, Bear said, "Time for you to tell me just who this Ghost is, don't you think? Now that I've joined the Sapienza family as Frankie's personal PI?"

Vinny turned sideways in the driver's seat and glanced back at his passenger. Bear could see the sharp planes of his chiseled face and the narrow aquiline nose. "You are not a member of the *famiglia, Signore* Bear. A friend, yes. Like Ghost. He ez specialist, resource we trust. Same with you. But *famiglia?* No."

Well, that settles that. Always the bridesmaid, never the bride.

Bear snorted to himself, glad not to be part of this tight knit mob. Fine by him. He still valued his rickety old carcass, and it would stay a damn sight safer out of the direct line of fire.

Vinny glanced at Bear again with eyes cold and grey as stone. Then he stared off into the woods. "Was year 1991. Ghost and me, we do, ah, special ops in Iraq. What they call counter-terrorism. *Capiche?* He moves with such stealth, unseen as a ghost. Gets his name that way."

"Good name. Ghost," Bear said. He'd been rather fond of his own nickname ever since a crazy old crock at the nursing home had thought he *was* a bear. He was a lot fatter and meaner back then. Now he liked to think of himself as merely big, as well as pleasant.

Vinny squared his jaw and continued to face down the past. "We placed explosive in enemy camp late one night. We could not know they had prisoners. Families. Families we were there to save. That night, they died by our hand. We left, silent as we came. But not Ghost. He stay behind. Frozen, you see, numb with guilt. The terrorists, they catch him. It goes bad for him until our team gets him back. Very bad. They ship him home and patch him together. But he still sees bodies of children who died that night. He keeps to himself now, wild in these woods for ten years. More. I bring him supplies time to time. We each have satellite phone. He has solar battery packs."

Bear rumbled a disgusted sigh deep in his throat. So many war stories with damaged veterans who do what their country asks. He shook his head and looked back out his window.

A wild man, in the green and brown of a woodland camo jacket, was staring in.

✦ ✦ ✦

Jessica Winslow was thrilled with the rare freedom of a whole day on her own. The sun was strong enough to warm the air billowing through her open window, her radio blared with old favorites, her horse trailer pulled easy behind the pick-up she'd borrowed from her barn manager, Sam. Her most experienced aide, Chrissie Metzger, was in charge of the five residents at Latin's Ranch.

TGFC. Thank God for Chrissie.

The aide had been with Jessica since Latin's Ranch opened, had even worked with the residents when they were still in a nursing home. She was a surprising young woman, one whose slouch and weak chin made her look defeated by life. But Chrissie was a rock. She knew the ins and outs of resident care, especially the fussy attention required by Lily's remaining leg. Chrissie's vigilance and diligence allowed Jessica these moments by herself to follow her favorite pursuit.

TGFC.

Jessica was on her way home from a horse meet that had been a small county affair. She had judged a dressage class and given a clinic on training Paso Finos. The truth was that the gaits that made the breed unique came pretty naturally to them. All the rider had to do was keep out of the way.

She'd taken both Latin Lover and the filly, Marisol. Latin had performed like the champion he was, impressing the crowd as she put him through his paces. He'd demonstrated the Paso Largo, his quickest gait this side of a full gallop. Then he wowed with his Classic Fino, four even-spaced steps in rapid rhythm that covered as little ground as possible. The motion was absorbed in Latin's back and loins so the ride for Jessica was exceptionally smooth. People with bad backs who couldn't ride any other breed could sometimes ride a Paso Fino. As she circled the ring, Jessica again thought how she'd like Lily to give it a try.

Marisol was too young to show, but Jessica wanted her to get used to crowds. She used the filly to demonstrate how to start with a blanket, then add a saddle without the cinch tightened and let the youngster get used to weight on its back. She would return for another clinic in the spring to show how to bridle and introduce a rider.

The crowd had been appreciative and the officials grateful. Latin had been a ham. All in all, Jessica was delighted. She made little at a show like this, but she liked the attention, and it could easily lead to a $1,500 stud fee or at least more customers for riding lessons.

As she drove home towing the horse trailer, Jessica could still feel the grin that had been plastered on her face most of the day. She reached up to push a blonde curl away from her eyes, and she began to sing loud and off key with the Dixie Chicks rocking on her radio.

Things had been so crazy for so long. The loss of her husband, the near failure of the ranch, the start-up of the adult care business, a new relationship. Ups and downs were coming at her with the speed of fast balls. Things were mostly good now ... but would it all go sour again?

Her five adult care residents seemed content. But how long before one fell or experienced an episode that wouldn't end with recovery? She'd actually made money on boarding and breeding horses this summer. But would another event like the feral dogs put an end to that? Ben Stassen was being a love, but would his daughter cause him to pull away for good?

Ah well. It was no use to worry. A sense of well-being settled on her like a soft shawl. It lasted until she got to the barn. That's when Lily and Sam met her.

"We have something to tell you," said Lily. If she'd had two legs, she might have dug a toe in the ground like a child confessing to breaking a cookie jar.

"*She* has something to tell you," said Sam. "I'll go unload the horses."

As Sam hustled off toward the horse trailer, Jessica felt her euphoria depart with him. She could see that Lily was upset from the way she leaned heavily on the walker. Jessica's teeth clenched. Her shawl of well-being was beginning to feel like a wet blanket.

CHAPTER THREE

Case Notes
September 17, 11 a.m.

Jessica took it pretty well. Oh, she used some unladylike phrases and threatened to boot our sorry asses from here to Puget Sound. It took all my awesome talent as a Peacemaker to settle her down. When I explained why Sam was giving up his trailer for a few days, I emphasized the importance of him being closer to the horses while dogs were on the prowl. I then assured her we had chosen the trailer to avoid imposing on anybody in the main house. That way, even if goons found Solana, we'd be safe. And, of course, I didn't tell Jessica the full horror of the story. I didn't lie; several details just slipped my mind, you know?

My real sales tool was Solana herself. Jessica stomped off to the trailer to hear her story face to face, and she was in no mood to put up with any nonsense. Solana managed to look even frailer than she had before. Worked a little tremble into her chin and hands. I do like that girl. You could see Jessica soften like butter in the sun. In the end, she agreed to three nights before she went to the authorities. She even had our youngest aide, Alita, deliver a tray of Aurora's crusty bread and chunky beef stew to the trailer.

Bear's right. Jess is putty in the hands of the helpless.

Speaking of Bear, he got back late from meeting with Ghost yesterday. I didn't have the chance to talk with him until this morning after Greek yogurt parfaits and mini-waffles with homemade black-berry jam. I admit Solana's story troubled me all night. I'm a tough old bird, but I felt terrified for her. I wanted to tell Bear all about it, but I could see he had his own issues ... he only had one helping at breakfast.

Meeting Ghost had upset him. A damaged soldier from the Middle East wars awakened memories of a whole different conflict for Bear. He waged war in Vietnam as a boy. In the 60s and 70s the people on the home front were just as confused as people are today about the rights and wrongs of the Middle East. We're angrier now, maybe because we've had too much experience with useless loss of life to pretend innocence anymore.

We learned a lot about Post Traumatic Stress Disorder back then. Long before 'Nam, it was called shell shock, and its victims were labeled cowards. War after war, we send off our eager young people, terrify them, teach them to kill, wound them physically and men-tally, then bring them home expecting them to fit right back inside society's narrow boundaries. Some make it. Others are always round pegs in a square life.

Bear went through it all, and some might say he's just okey-dokey. But I know his struggles with personal relationships, including a failed marriage and a career of working on his own instead of with close associates. War can be an overwhelming reason to never trust again. I should know, what with being a war widow myself. My hus-band's remains are still in 'Nam. There wasn't enough left to send home to his young wife and his baby, Sylvia.

Anyhoo, my mind is wandering, probably to avoid dwelling on Sola-na's story. And I must get to it. PTSD can affect a damaged woman like Solana as much as it can a soldier. And every bit of it is due to man's inhumanity to man. The more things change, right?

I volunteered Bear and me to fold the week's clean towels. It would give us some quiet time together.

- Lily Gilbert, Stressed Assistant to PI Bear Jacobs

Lily and Bear were at the game table in the living room nearly hidden by a warm fluffy mountain of towels fresh from the dryer. Neither was feeling sociable with anyone other than each other. The big man had finally told her about his meeting with Ghost. His outrage was palpable. "The guy's thin as a rake. Missing a couple front teeth. Smells like a garbage truck. Sores and scars on every visible inch of skin like Mother Nature's giving him tats. Vinny says he's been taught things and done things that humans should never know. I'd say he's wary as an alley cat. Spooky posture, ready to pounce. Other than that and, oh yea, those injured eyes, he's a regular guy. Somebody the average family would love to invite into their home. A hero of the foreign wars."

Lily tried to placate. "He's where he wants to be, Bear."

"Yeah, right."

"Okay, where he needs to be then."

"Yeah. Living where he's no threat to civilization. Or more accurate, where civilization can't hurt him anymore."

Lily finished folding a baker's dozen then sat back in her chair waiting for Bear to catch up. He was on towel number one. She was giving him time to calm down before she raised his blood pressure again with Solana's story.

Out of the corner of her eye, she noticed the mound of unfolded laundry begin to quiver just as the big man reached for a second towel. "Wait!" But she was too late. An orange paw shot out of the pile and slashed at Bear's hand with the bravado of an experienced swordsman.

"What the ...?" Bear examined his fist for scratches as the totality of Furball appeared, meowed, jumped to the floor, lifted his magnificent tail skyward and sashayed out of the room. On his way, he hissed at the caged canaries just to keep them on their toes.

At least Furball had gotten Bear's attention away from Ghost. Lily seized the moment. "I do care about Ghost, Bear. But I need to tell you what happened to Solana before she met up with him. To keep events in order in my mind. I have to get this said."

Bear cocked his head at her. She picked up a towel to fold, but ended holding it against her chest. Warmth for a cold shiver.

Watching her, Bear was suddenly all attention. "Tell me, Lily."

She began in a voice as unsteady as a loose string. "I need to tell you what Solana told Eunice and me. Once she got started, she had a lot to say. The girl's good with details. Even the ugly ones." Lily swallowed back a lump of distress and struggled on. "Solana was snatched from the homeless camp where she and her sister Rosie live. Out there near the county park. She was in a nearby meadow picking blackberries when she was grabbed from behind, gagged, and given some kind of injection. Whatever it was, she blacked out right after that."

"She didn't see who attacked?" Bear's attention was complete. His hands reached for another towel, but Lily knew when he was slow like this, motion deliberate and contained, he was listening intently.

Lily shook her head. "Didn't have the chance. She became conscious at one point, though, enough to hear a high pitched engine whine. A blindfold kept her from seeing. She could feel motion but not like a car or boat. More like being in the air only dippier. It made her vomit. Someone yelled, 'Fucking bitch,' loud enough that she heard it over the engine noise, then she was given another injection."

"Helicopter?"

"I assume." Lily consulted the notes on her laptop. She'd placed it on the chair beside her where she could see the screen. Everyone knew Lily's little Toshiba was rarely far from her reach.

She took another deep breath. The next part was so very hard. "When Solana came to again, she was alone. She wasn't tied or blindfolded anymore. She saw metal bars and thought she might be in a cell. But the bars weren't as thick as that. As her focus cleared, she saw her enclosure was actually a cage, about the size of a kennel for a St. Bernard. She'd been lying on a mat under a blanket. She could sit but there wasn't room to stand." Lily looked up from her notes. "A dog kennel, Bear. They put her in a dog kennel."

Her old friend grunted as if sucker punched. He touched her slender shoulder. This amounted to intense commiseration from Bear. "Was she injured? Are you? Do you want to stop? You don't have to do this, Lily."

"I'm okay, Bear. You have to hear this from me, because she'll never tell you face to face. Not sure she'll trust any man ever again." Lily sniffed and picked up the story again. "She looked herself over and didn't have so much as a bruise. She felt a huge wave of relief for that. Maybe her captors didn't intend to hurt her, just scare her. Next, she looked past the cage bars to her surroundings beyond. It was a tiny room with plain cinder block walls. Nothing else was in it except three other cages just like hers, all lined up along one wall. Two were empty. In the last one, a 'black dude' was staring back at her. 'Black dude' was her term for him."

"Did she recognize him?" Bear had managed to fold the towel in half.

"She'd never seen him before. He looked 'sorta old' to her, so make that middle-aged. To her, Eunice and I are ancients. He'd just called to her, asking if she was all right, when she heard a man's voice in another room say 'Go get the spook, Ape. I hear him in there.' Three guys came in then. One had a gun, a 'big gun' was her only way to describe it. They opened Black Dude's cage, ordered him out and walked him away. To Solana, he looked as frightened as she felt."

Lily looked up from her notes, worry lines gathering to create a new wrinkle between her eyebrows. "And Bear, they made no effort to hide their faces from her."

"Oooff," he expelled a slow breath. "I assume she's seen enough movies to know what that means."

Lily nodded. "She knew then that they had no intention of letting her go. It petrified her. She panicked, started to scream. It wasn't long before the one called Ape came back. She says he looks like an orangutan. Wild red hair, big chest, jutting jaw. He waved a switchblade and told her to shut her yap or he'd fill it for her. He made an obscene gesture grabbing his privates. She curled back up on the mat, covered herself with the blanket and sobbed as quietly as she could."

Bear completed the final fold, snapping it with force. "How did she escape?"

"They must not have expected any more trouble from her. She does look too fragile to have much fight in her. The three goons came back later and told her to get out of the cage. She refused. Ape reached in and pulled her out by her hair. They stood in a ring around her and made her strip. When she was naked, two of them held her down so she couldn't move while Ape ..."

Lily couldn't continue. She began folding towels with a vengeance, until most of the snowy mountain was reduced to flat stacks. She wanted to snatch the washcloth out of Bear's hands, but he seemed attached to it. Finally, she got herself under control. "After he was done, he told the others, 'She's all yours. But be goddamn sure you don't leave any marks or there'll be hell to pay.' Then he left. The other two guys began to bicker about who went next. Their language got, well, I don't need to repeat it. They started to fight. Solana realized this distraction was her only chance. While they snarled at each other, she got up. They didn't notice as she crept toward the doorway. And then she ran.

"When she got out of the room she saw that she was in an open building, maybe a warehouse or small hangar. It was dark, and she remembers being glad because she was still naked. The only lights were bright overheads hung at the far end of the building. There was enough dust in the air for the beams to spotlight a set, like a play. She could see silhouettes of people walking around in front of it.

"Solana figured she must be so scared that she was losing her mind. Nothing made sense. Two guys dressed in white sheets and pointy hats like the KKK were standing there talking to another guy with a clip board. The scene lit by the overheads had a gnarled dead tree. A noose was hanging from it. Then Solana saw Black Dude in another cage. She felt her way along the dark wall unnoticed until she got close to a huge bay door, the kind where big trucks load. It was open. Men were carrying in scenery for movies or plays. Stage sets.

"Solana thought she could escape while they were busy. But she hesitated because it's hard to go unnoticed when you're naked. Then she heard someone behind her yell, 'Bitch got away. Find her.' Solana ducked into another side room."

"Sounds like the place was equipped as a film studio," Bear muttered. "Actually, the whole story sounds like a bad movie plot."

"The room she was in was small. Racks of clothes filled most of it. They were costumes – cop uniforms and bar maid corsets. She hid among the racks and grabbed stuff to cover herself. Happened to be a cowboy shirt and basketball shorts. Then she crammed her feet into some sort of sandals. Meanwhile, she heard people in the main room yelling and running past the wardrobe door. After they passed, she peeked out.

"Nobody was in sight except Black Dude in the cage. She ran over to open it, but it was padlocked. He said to her, 'Go. Hide. They think you've escaped outside. Hide under the first thing you find so they don't see you on their way back.'

"Solana hesitated. She didn't want to leave him, but she couldn't open the padlock. He ordered her to go. "You're no good to me here. Find help if you can." So she ran to the garage door. There were lights on the outside of the building but it was blackness beyond. Damp. Smelled of mold and wet earth. She heard men yelling for her. Things like, 'come back now and we won't hurt you. If you don't …' well, you know the kind of threat.

"She dashed into the woods and hid under a stand of salal bushes. When the search party came back, she heard one voice say they'd look again in daylight. Another added she'd probably die of exposure by then. Once they were back inside, she took off. She figured she could get a few hours ahead of them. But she was moving blind with only a little moonlight to help. She's had some experience with roughing it in the wild, so maybe that saved her. But it was slow going.

"She was on the run for two days before she heard them catching up behind her. Likely she'd been going in circles. Whatever, she was too exhausted to go much farther."

When Lily came to a halt with a sigh, Bear picked up the narrative. "Two days. Jesus. That must be about when Ghost saw her. She was weaving through the woods this way and that. It actually made her harder for those bastards to follow since there was no logic in her motions. Ghost backtracked far enough to see three men through the trees a couple hundred yards behind her. He returned double speed to where she was struggling along. He found her just as she'd looked over her shoulder and run her head smack into a limb. He couldn't revive her so he picked her up and carried her to a place near a creek where they could hide. Some kind of cavern carved out of the bank by the water."

Lily cut back in. "Yes. That's where she came to. He scared the crap out of her. But not as much as the others had, so she didn't put up a huge fight against him. Probably too exhausted anyway."

"Ghost said that on the way to a safer place, she mentioned the name of Ape. He'd heard it before. That's why he called Vinny."

Lily was appalled. "You mean to tell me *Vinny* knows these thugs?"

"Vinny *is* a thug, Lily, so yeah, he knows a few others. He figures Ape is a strange enough nickname that there's not likely two of them in the area. Joey the Ape is an enforcer from another family. The only people who dare to call him Ape to his face are higher on the pecking order than he is. Vinny says it's a family that Frankie detests."

At last, Bear whipped the washcloth into shape with precise folds. In his enormous hands, it looked the size of a centennial stamp. "Next day Ghost took Solana to a spot in the woods where Vinny could pick her up. He had one of the *famiglia* doctors see to her, then took her to Fred Meyer to buy some clothes. All she had were the cowboy shirt and basketball shorts she'd taken from the wardrobe room. And they were in tatters."

Lily felt something shift inside. Hysteria loosening its grip? She nearly laughed at the idea of a young girl shopping with Vinny in tow. Fred Meyer probably wasn't used to hit men in the juniors department. She stuffed the emotion back down and asked, "So you think whatever is going on out there is related to mob activity?"

"I think we need another talk with Frankie."

When Bear lumbered off to request an audience, he'd only completed a handful of towels, but they were military masterpieces. Sharp, straight, even creases.

Old soldiers.

Then Lily finished folding all the rest.

✦   ✦   ✦

Bennett Stassen was a worried man. Apprehension was rare for him since he was usually solid as a rock. He'd been a friend of Ed Winslow until he'd died, leaving Jessica to go it alone. Ben's affections had easily landed on the young widow, and he was there when her grief finally lifted enough for her to see him. Now he was her lover and, he hoped, someday her husband. He didn't actually live at Latin's Ranch yet, but he spent nearly every night there. His own condo had become little more than an office and mailing address.

In his earlier days, Ben had been dumped by a wandering wife. He could have recovered from that without a lot of ill will. But when she pranced away, she also left their daughter, Rachael. The kid had turned mean as a weasel. She'd become a paid-in-full member of the Seattle street culture until the day, four months back, when she'd turned up at Latin's Ranch, hugely pregnant and begging for sanctuary. Jessica provided the one vacant room she had in the home, and Ben paid for it.

His daughter was a mystery to Ben. But this baby. This baby was no mystery at all. This was love. And this was worry.

Was the baby an addict? Cocaine? Marijuana? Was he a crack baby? A test on Rachael's urine had suggested the possibility. How long had Rachael been using while pregnant? She claimed she'd quit once she knew. If it was true, the baby had a good chance of recovery. But Ben knew Rachael lied when it was convenient.

Drugs could cross the placenta, cause long term learning and behavior problems in the baby. The little boy had been a preemie but not by too many weeks. Maybe he could fight off all the symptoms of withdrawal. It was too soon to know.

He looked calm enough right now, all pink and asleep in Ben's arms, wispy black locks sticking out from a blue sequined cap that Eunice had crocheted and decorated. But he was often fussy, crying as though his little heart was aching.

Would this baby ever have a name? So far it was Baby Boy Stassen because Rachael couldn't decide between Bono and Eminem. She named no one as the father, just made bad jokes about immaculate conception. Would she ever take this responsibility seriously?

Bennett Stassen was a worried man.

CHAPTER FOUR

Case Notes
September 17, 4 p.m.

Frankie Sapienza is the only one of us with a private room. Eunice and I share, as do Charlie and Bear. Charlie, Bear and I all receive Medicaid so we don't qualify for private rooms, and Eunice would rather share than be by herself. It works out fine, maybe because the four of us lived together at the Soundside nursing home before transferring here.

The other single room has been reserved for another private pay customer. Jessica has not yet found the person that she wants, and we're just as glad. To be honest, the rest of us would like a veto power over the candidate. The balance of these things is delicate. Our little family works because not one of us is a chucklehead.

But Ben's daughter Rachael comes close. Jessica has allowed her the private room until she can get back on her feet and decide what lies ahead for her and her baby. As far as I can tell, the girl's doing no planning whatsoever.

That may not be good for Baby Boy, but it's okay with us. Old people, other than Charlie who sleeps like a noisy log, are insomniacs. At least one of us is up in the night reading, computing, watching Seinfeld reruns. It took Rachael about half a second to realize she could change and feed Baby Boy, plop him onto one of our laps and return to bed. He's a fussy baby, cries often, but we're content to rock

*him into a better mood. We hold him until Ben gets up in the early
hours to go to work. He changes BB, gives him a bottle, burps him,
puts him back in his crib. If Chrissie is the aide on duty, she helps.
What with two rug rats of her own, she knows which end of a baby
is which. Rick and Alita, our other aides, seem totally befuddled by
helping anyone too young for Medicare.*

*Cradling a fat little ball of life, comforting his cries and tickling his
tummy, makes each of us feel useful again. Ben worries that maybe
BB fusses too much or is too hard to comfort which could be signs of
addiction. Imagine the gauntlet this little person has run through all
of his mother's bad habits. The possibilities defeat me, so I choose to
love him now and not think of his future.*

*With all our help, Rachael gets her beauty sleep. Too bad it doesn't
do much for her moods. Well, okay, that's a little unfair. She has been
clean and sober while she's been here. But it is a constant battle for
her, and she is more than willing to let the rest of us know it. Even
Jessica's dog Folly steers clear, and Folly likes everyone.*

*Hearing a baby cry late in the night is a new noise at Latin's Ranch.
We hadn't realized how much we've missed such a sound.*

- Lily Gilbert, Babysitting Assistant to PI Bear Jaco

Bear had seen Frankie's room because men could enter the inner sanctum from time to time. But it would be new territory for Lily. He warned her in advance that she should take her lead from him. "Don't get in a hissy fit with him. He's a mobster from the old world with no concept of sexual equality."

"Okay. I'll save my hissy fit for you."

"Great," he muttered before knocking on the door.

Frankie's room was not particularly large, especially considering the size of his handcrafted Italianate furniture. The jacquard bedding and matching ivory drapes were not standard issue, nor was the classic side table – inlaid and accented with gold – that doubled as his nightstand.

By the time chairs big enough for Bear and Vinny had been arranged, and room created for Lily's wheelchair along with Frankie's walker, it was a convalescent traffic jam. Vinny opened the patio door to let in some sunshine and fresh air. Each resident room had a glass door because it qualified as an emergency exit. Bear noticed Vinny seat himself where he could watch that opening, lest thugs from some enemy camp attempt a takeover.

Bear sniffed in a deep breath of air spiced with moist evergreen and the drier musk of leaves coming to the end of their lifespan. This crystalline day was the kind that people felt was their due for putting up with all the Seattle rain. Bear hoped this meeting would do as much to clear his mystified head.

Things started as rocky as he had anticipated. Frankie balked at the very idea of Lily attending. A lady did not belong in a gentleman's bedroom. Bear countered that she kept his notes and assisted his investigations. He swore she would stay quiet while they spoke of business which was, of course, a topic only for men. The old Sicilian finally acquiesced although he was clearly nonplused. Even the stone-faced Vinny raised an eyebrow.

Lily sat with her computer on a lapboard, ready to start. Bear knew she'd play her role, but he couldn't keep himself from saying, "Now keep your yap shut."

Bear brought Frankie and Vinny up to speed with the story as told by Solana and Ghost. Then he stated his conclusions. "They're making movies somewhere deep in the woods. You'd first think kiddie porn with a set up like that. But the two kidnapped people we know about so far are an of-age girl and an adult black male. So this isn't about children. Plus, they've got wardrobe out there. Solana was wearing a cowboy shirt and basketball shorts that she grabbed from racks just to cover herself. Sandals from some kind of goddess get-up. And she saw men in KKK costumes."

Vinny fidgeted, jangling change in his pocket. Or nail clippers against bullets. Or a knife against lock picks. Bear knew the bodyguard wasn't good at taking it easy, that he'd be happier with his hands around someone's neck.

"The other thing we know is that their victims can't have wounds that show. They talked about that, about not 'marking' them. Even when they raped Solana, they held her still. Didn't bruise her arms or face. Strange behavior for kidnappers. So, Frankie. What can you tell us about what's going on?"

Frankie's old face was still handsome for an eighty-something with strong Italian bones, brilliant white teeth, and a full head of salt and pepper hair. Most days, he fit with the other residents just fine. Everyone liked him. But now his dark eyes pierced Bear with the intensity of a raptor.

Bear switched to his just-this-side-of-a-growl voice. "Come on, Frankie. You haven't told me all you know. One thing for sure, you didn't involve me in this just to wet nurse a teenage girl. This isn't about Solana. She's only the spur that goaded you to action. There's something bigger here, something seriously rotten. And you know what."

With no other body motion, Frankie cut his steely gaze over to Vinny. Some kind of bad guy code passed between them. Bear knew a little of that language, having dealt with the underbelly of society in his earlier life. He felt a chill. Whether it was from the open door or the Sicilians, he couldn't say.

"*Merda*," Frankie muttered. "You are right. There ez more. Vinny, you tell why I am here. Leave out nothing. *Niente.*"

Bear knew Vinny was not used to center stage, being far more comfortable in the darkened wings. But the bodyguard cleared his throat and began. "*Signore* Sapienza has grandson. Antonio, the man who brought him here."

"Yes, Tony!" Lily said.

All three men stared at her.

"Ah, Tony Sapienza is a friend of my daughter, Sylvia." Her voice trailed off then she returned to her notes, computer keys clacking.

Vinny's gaze lingered on her briefly while Frankie said, "The leaders in newer gangs search for me because I am head of the Sapienza family. You may have guessed at that."

Bear couldn't look at Lily for fear they'd snicker and roll their eyes. The capo had no idea just how often speculation about him had been the evening's entertainment.

Bear didn't miss the shake in Frankie's gnarled hands. A tremor? No, anger. That was obvious when the old man spit out the word, "*Bastardos!*" Lily, Bear and even Vinny noticeably jumped. In a quieter tone, one a snake might use, Frankie continued. "They wish to eliminate me. They think we are weak because I am old. They want our business, no? So I hide here. Only Tony and Vinny know where. And now you two."

"Right. I get it. Who'd look for a gangland kingpin on a geriatric's horse ranch."

"*Precisamente.*" Frankie bowed slightly toward Bear.

The residents had always known that Frankie had a vastly different background from their own. It had been fun to wonder about the mob, but this was for real. The old don's presence might have consequences for them all. His safety could put the rest of them in danger.

"The *Signore*, he hates what the new gangs do to good family business," Vinny said. "Drugs. Slave trade. Now this. He has told you this much. This ez why he hires you, *Signore* Bear."

"I don't know," Bear said with a slow swing of his head side to side. "You have a helluva lot more resources than I do."

Frankie nodded. "But not for this. One of my own *famiglia* asking questions? That could be traced back to me. So I hire you. To help us stop this awful thing."

Bear's bullshit alarm rang. Frankie might be appalled by a sick crime. But the don was also aware that if the crime came under public scrutiny, so would all the gangs. Not good for business.

Before Bear spoke his thought, Frankie continued with a shrug of his narrow shoulders. "This girl found by Ghost, she fingers Joey the Ape. You have a place to begin. You already are putting together clues."

"You know who he is?"

Frankie confirmed with the slightest of nods. "We know the gang he works for. Not something for you to worry about."

Bear tugged at a handful of hairs on his beard. "So I provide the info and you, ah, shall we say, intend to shut the operation down?"

The room was still other than the tick of an antique Imperial mantel clock and the tap of Lily's keys. Outside, birds twittered and Folly growled at a toy, probably his favorite rope bone. "We do not like to speak of such things aloud," Frankie finally said. "This ez evil, this return of snuff films."

When Lily gasped, all three men stared at her again. Her pink suede-like skin had gone white. "Snuff films?" she exploded. "You mean movies where someone is murdered? Snuffed out? I thought they were urban legends. And forgive me all to hell and gone for speaking up in the men's room."

Bear touched her arm.

"I'm okay, damn it. Continue." Lily returned to her computer, but Bear figured the tears in her eyes made the keys hard to see.

"Ez okay, Miss Lily. Ez a very bad thing we discuss."

I'll be damned. An olive branch from the don.

Bear stepped back into the conversation. "Haven't heard about snuff films lately, Lily, but they're real. Too sick to surface often."

Lily placed a hand on her Toshiba, lowering its lid as if to protect it. The noise she made sounded like a moan to Bear. He was rattled by her distress. And by his own. This was getting far too big for a fat old cripple. He would fail. In shame and surrender he said, "It's time to involve the law, Frankie."

The Sicilian waved his hand wildly. "This cannot be, Bear. The law may find the movie makers. But these are little people. *Mi famiglia* will cut off the monster's head when you reveal it."

"I have to contact the authorities, Frankie. You don't have to worry because they probably won't believe me. But I've worked on the side of the law all my life. I may skirt it now and then, but at the end of the day, without rules society is just chaos."

Frankie dropped his hand to his lap. He exchanged another glance with Vinny, then he shook his head with a sigh. "I do not understand you people who do not leave such things as retribution to your families. If you must notify the authorities, then promise me three things."

He raised one bony finger then another and another. "First, you will take great care. There are bad guys among the ranks of the good guys. You understand? And two. There will be no mention of my name or my family. And three. You will not stop me from doing the things I must do. Agree?"

It was Bear and Lily's turn to exchange another glance. Lily nodded at him. He turned back to Frankie and reluctantly said, "Agreed. But I tell my other operatives, too."

"And that is?"

"Charlie and Eunice."

"Ah, yes." Frankie finally nodded. "I will talk to my little dove, as well.

She must know the man I am."

Vinny stood. "*Mi Signore*, his safety depends on you now. In return, you depend on Vinny."

Bear sighed. Life under the wing of a thug. You just never can tell what each new day will bring.

✦ ✦ ✦

Lily wondered if a brain could suffer arrhythmia the same way a heart could get out of whack. Hers felt too aflutter to process data.

First, the speculations of a don in their midst was no longer just fun. It turned out to be fact. And then snuff films. A real murder for God's sake. Lily was exhausted by the time she and Bear had rolled and limped from the don's room to the sunny living room, more from emotions than from wheeling her chair with her hands. "You could watch your little bit of filth whenever you were feeling low. Or powerless. Or however you'd have to feel to watch something like that. What the hell is happening to civilization, Bear?"

"Don't know, Lily." He collapsed into his favorite overstuffed chair. The living room had wide open spaces as if the furniture had been shoved against the walls for a dance. Actually, it was so wheelchairs and walkers could easily spin and turn. "Lots of us are born to be monsters. Look at our history. Left unfettered, humans invent iron maidens or practice genocide or use their young as sex toys. All that evil backs up from time to time like a sewer line. Blows the lid off whatever crust of civilization we've managed to construct."

"But why now? I know people are angry about terrorism and school shootings and dirty politicians and who's moving in next door. But mad enough to watch actual murders? Enough for it to be profitable entertainment?"

"Yes. That much madness."

Lily realized being a private investigator's assistant meant dipping lower into the muck than she'd ever gone before.

Should I tell Bear I don't want to do this anymore? Should I just try to be happy in the few years I have left? Garden? Write a story?

He read her mind. "Do you want to stop now, Lily? It would be acceptable if you do."

She waffled. Yes, she wanted to stop, to never look under the rug again. Turn her back. "We can't stop, Bear. We have to fight back, in our own way. If only because Baby Boy will live in this world long after we're gone."

"That he will. That he will."

Precisely at four, Charlie joined them. Lily poured tea from the afternoon service set out on the game table. She also plated the puffy sopapillas still warm from the fryer and set one in front of each of them. After licking powdered sugar from her fingertips Lily added, "We have some things to tell you."

"Like what?" Charlie asked, raising his thin voice over the thunderous purr of Furball, the cat curled in his lap. "Hurry it up. I wanted to watch my pawn shop show."

"It's only the fourteenth rerun," Lily muttered.

"Look at this!" Eunice said, scuttling into the room juggling a huge sewing bag under one arm while holding up a dark blue baby sweater. The number 12 emblazoned it in lime green sequins. "Now BB is a real Seattle sports fan."

"Um, nice Eunice. Made it yourself, did you?"

"Why yes, Bear. Glad you recognize true artistry. Maybe I could whip one up for you." She dumped the floral patterned bag on a cushy chair and rummaged out a measuring tape. "Now let's see ..."

He held up a hand in Smokey Bear fashion. "Thanks, but no thanks, Eunice. A bear can't wear Seahawk attire."

"Oh, well, I suppose not." She flopped down beside her sewing bag and held up the little sweater again to admire for herself. "Maybe he needs matching britches and a cap."

Bear turned back to Charlie as Lily was pouring tea for Eunice.

"We need to tell you two what's been going on. Might even take precedence over pawned goods or baby clothes." He then recounted the conversation with Frankie. As he talked, Charlie and Eunice frowned in concentration, at least until Charlie couldn't swallow his indignation any longer.

"Turning murder into a goddamn business?" He blurted while scratching his head which disrupted his comb over. His soft jowls folded into an even sadder tragedy mask than usual. He cupped his hands around Furball, hugging the fat old tomcat. Furball, interested in nobody's comfort but his own, broke loose and jumped down.

Lily noticed that Eunice had gone dead quiet, collapsing in on herself. But that delicate old spirit was marshalling its forces. A flush of anger traveled up Eunice's wrinkled neck from the swirls of her neon silk scarf to her already rouged cheeks. It finally burst free. "So that's why Solana was taken? Those bastards wanted to beat her to death just so someone could watch? Add a movie to their collection? That's ... that's ..." Eunice had worked her way to an octave that would shatter dog ears.

Lily took her hand, careful not to hurt those little bird bones. "That's outrageous. Yes, you're absolutely right. They found Solana by raiding her homeless camp. I imagine they stalk the street scene and soup kitchens for other victims. Nobody much cares when these people disappear."

A tear worked its way through the grooves of Eunice's eye wrinkles as she clutched the baby clothes in one hand and Lily's hand in the other. "And you think my Frankie is a part of this? That's even more –"

" – No, Eunice, no," Bear said. "Your Frankie is the good guy here. He's upset by all this, too. He's the one who brought it to my attention. He has things to tell you. He wants it stopped."

"Well, all right then," Eunice extracted her hand and wiped her eyes. "Let's stop it."

"What are you going to do?" Charlie asked Bear.

"What are *we* going to do?" Eunice asked.

Lily considered Bear's operatives. A willing old man with painful privates, an erstwhile beauty queen and a one-legged woman tapping away on her computer keys. Bear himself needed a quad cane and a frequent rest.

What the hell is *he gonna do?*

✦ ✦ ✦

Sylvia Henderson and Tony Sapienza were sharing four-adjective coffee in their local Starbuck's. She realized he considered himself her fashion consultant now that Kyle was no longer available. Kyle had been her husband and Tony's lover. His death had left both of them bereft, and on that fragile thread of shared grief, they had woven a strong and lasting friendship.

"It's not the color, Syl," he said. "Your auburn's fine. But you need to let it grow a little longer. Let it move in a breeze. Less spray, more play, you know? Loosen up, love." He sipped his grande iced skinny vanilla latte then continued with his critique. "And about your booty. You have a great ass for jeans. Why all these straight legged trousers? You've got it, girl, so go ahead and decorate it. Time for you to get back out there."

Tony's opinions could piss her off, but she trusted him to tell her the truth. She knew he worried about her being alone. "I *am* getting out there," she said defensively. "I went to a movie just the other night."

"By yourself?"

"Well, yes. And that was hard enough," she admitted. Sylvia did all right during the day when she was up to her elbows in Henderson interior design projects. But the nights were hard. Friendly couples had been generous with their time, inviting her to dinners and plays, but she was tired of feeling like a third-wheel charity case. Tony had started to circulate again, and she knew she needed to do the same if only to get him – and her mother, Lily – off her back. But going out by herself made her feel lonelier than being on her own at home.

"At least it's a start," Tony said, smiling at her. "What did you see?"

"That movie about the penguins. Cute."

He rolled his eyes. "For the love of God, Sylvia, the only men at movies like that are loaded down with kiddies already. You need man movies. Shoot 'em ups, car chases, easy women, simple plots. Every multiplex has them."

"I was seeing a movie, not hunting for a man, Tony. But speaking of men, I saw your grandfather's, ah, friend? ... employee? ... there. Vinny

Tononi. With a couple kiddies of his own." She munched a tiny piece of maple scone and tried to arrange her features to appear nonchalant. "Is he married?"

"Not Vinny. Must have been with his nephews." If a lightning bolt had struck him in the eye, Tony couldn't have lit up any more suddenly. "Don't tell me you're interested in *Vinny*? Not that he isn't as machismo as they come. OMG, Syl!"

"No, of course not. I'm not interested in anybody. Kyle was enough for me."

"Vinny would be more than enough for anyone. But your mother would crucify me for introducing you to a good fella. Get Vinny out of your fantasies right now."

"Tony, I'm forty-something. My mother doesn't approve men for me. And neither do you."

"That's right. You're only forty-something. So why you persist in dressing like a blue-hair, I don't know." With that, they were back to the fashion battle.

When she got home, she wondered if Tony might have a point, as she removed her chic Calvin Klein wool. She had to admit it was classy, but not much fun.

I wonder if people say that about me? Classy but not much fun.

She always dressed in fashion vs. fad. It was not just her preference. She thought it made a statement to her clients regarding the type of elegant interiors they could expect from her design. She put on a white terry robe, then picked up the bedside photo of her husband and asked, "What do you think, Kyle? Is it time for me to strut my stuff?"

Kyle had been gay. Or, rather, bisexual. She could say it now when, all their married life, it had been the only unspoken subject between them. They'd cuddled frequently, had sex less often. It had not been the raging hormone kind of carnage but a sweet and gentle affirmation of love between two people who accept anything from each other. It had been enough for her then. When Kyle died, Sylvia had wanted to go, too. Only Jessica's nurturing and her mother's increasing need and Tony's grief brought her back from a bleak nothingness.

Kyle smiled back at her, his eyes focused on hers in this, her favorite photo of him. He told her he believed it was time. She was not to mourn forever.

"Easy for you to say," she said. "But just a sec. I have something to show you." She went to her lingerie chest, opened the second drawer and reached far to the back for a raspberry colored push-up bra, a wisp of weightless silk. The matching thong had bits of lace supporting a triangle with about the same coverage as a Post-It note. Sylvia dangled the ensemble from two fingers for Kyle's consideration.

"Yes, they *are* mine," she cooed, thrusting a shapely hip to the side. "I bought them online at My Fair Pair. I guess I'm not as stuffy as you and Tony think. So there."

She looked at the frivolous undies then sighed as she sat on the edge of her bed. She'd never wear them, of course. They belonged in the most private depths of her lingerie drawer, and that is where they would stay. They were nothing more than the result of a wild impulse on a day when 'a sweet and gentle affirmation of love' was apparently not enough.

She wished she'd stop having these embarrassing dreams about Vinny Tononi ripping them off her quivering body as she reclined on a heart shaped bed.

CHAPTER FIVE

Case Notes
September 18, 9 a.m.

Rachael had opted not to breast feed Baby Boy, which was just as well since her milk was likely laden with enough chemicals for a drug lord to OD. My favorite aide Chrissie had changed BB into a onesie, and Bear was holding him, feeding him a bottle. The baby was making little piggy noises, and Bear was responding in kind. The two of them are developing a language all their own. Who'd have guessed the old fart would be so easily wooed by a young fart? Life can still surprise you, even when eighty is in sight. Reason enough to feel overjoyed I didn't follow up on suicide back when the road ahead looked entirely too bumpy.

Speaking of surprises. We heard a knock at the back door in the kitchen and Aurora call, "Entra." Moments later she ushered Solana into the dining room where we were finishing breakfast. The girl had her Fred Meyer shopping bags packed and ready, but Aurora sat her down at the table with a short stack of blueberry cakes and bacon. Nobody gets past Aurora without a good meal.

Solana looked shyly at the residents around the table and picked me out to address her comments. "I'm leaving now and wanted to say thank you."

"You're leaving?" Frankie, Eunice and I sounded like an a cappella

trio. Charlie looked up as he poured more syrup on his pancakes. Bear continued to chortle and snort with BB.

"You can't leave," said Eunice. "You're safer here than on the road."

Solana shot the pugnacious scowl of the young around the table. "I have to get back to Rosie. I'm afraid she's in danger."

Bear said, "You're right. She is."

That simple statement shut us all up. It made my blood run cold. With a trembling lip, Solana finally said, "Maybe I can go get her and bring her back here with me?"

Bear shook his head. "No, you can't. But I can."

Solana's eyes, pooling over with tears, opened wide. "But you're ... you're ..."

"Yes, I'm old and walk with a cane and that makes me as useless as last year's calendar. But I know how to save your sister. You have a picture of her?"

"Yes, but ..."

"She look like you?"

"Yes, but ..."

"Then give it to me. Tell me exactly where the homeless camp is, then write a note that Rosie will know came from you. Tell her to go with the woman who shows it to her."

Solana began to write on the back of a paper napkin. Bear handed BB to Eunice, got up and kachunk, kachunked out of the room with the help of his quad cane. He was humming Someone to Watch Over Me. He does that, you know. Hums old hits when he's thinking. I pushed back my chair, grabbed for my walker and followed him to destinations unknown.

- Lily Gilbert, *Tag Along Assistant to PI Bear Jacobs*

"Where to?" Lily asked.

"Lots to do," Bear answered. "First, we have to find that girl, Rosie. We'll go strong arm Sam. Get something warm, then meet me at Sitting Bull."

Sitting Bull was their mode of short-range transportation, provided by Eunice's ample bank account. She'd wanted them all to be able to roam the Latin's Ranch acreage freely, but with their various handicaps and fragile bones, they couldn't exactly hike. Or handle Harleys. Sitting Bull was the solution. It was a golf cart custom-made to be street worthy, and any of them could drive it since there were no foot controls. The candy apple steed held two in front with a passenger seat that swung out for easy access from a wheelchair or walker. The back seat faced forward, too, so a person could sit next to a folded wheelchair. Or a fourth could ride along if the gang wasn't toting their mobility equipment.

Sitting Bull's customization made it legal on roads with speed limits up to 35 mph. That was at least five miles per hour faster than the thing could go when really maxed out. The gang rarely used it off the ranch if for no other reason than it gave Jessica clammy hands, frayed nerves and cold sweats all at the same time. Besides, most places were too far away. But the real reason? While Bear would venture out occasionally, only Eunice still had a valid license. And nobody wanted her at the wheel on the open road.

"We need it at that homeless camp," Bear said to Lily as she lifted herself into the passenger seat, then wrapped her shoulders in a plaid throw. "Sitting Bull is the only way to handle a trail through the woods for you and me. Neither of us is Fred Astaire on our pins anymore."

"Maybe I could bunny hop," one-legged Lily muttered.

Bear unplugged the Bull, folded Lily's walker into the back seat and placed his quad cane next to it. Then he plopped heavily into the driver's seat. "I believe that comment is the type youngsters call snarky," he said as they glided silently toward the barn.

Lily had plans regarding her condition, but now wasn't the time to think about it. They passed the Airstream and the riding ring, continuing on in search of Jessica's barn manager, Sam Hart. He had a small flat-bed trailer that he used for hauling hay, loads of cedar curls for the stalls, sacks of grain, whatever needed to get from one place to the next. That included Sitting Bull every now and then.

"Sam won't be easy to convince, even for you," Lily said. She knew all about Bear's occasional gift of cigars or whiskey. And the poker nights the two of them held in Sam's trailer. They were friends. Bear could probably bring Sam around, but he'd gotten the taciturn man in trouble before. "He won't be eager to do something that could distress Jessica."

"You mean like drop a couple of her crackpot residents off at a county park?"

"Yeah, like that."

They succeeded with Sam, but it took working as a tag team. While they explained what they needed, he was mucking out Gina Lola's stall. The dappled gray Percheron mare swayed her massive head from person to person as they spoke, looking like a spectator at the world's slowest tennis match.

"No effing way am I driving you out to that county park," Sam said. "And pardon my language there, Miss Lily."

"It's broad daylight and nothing dangerous," Bear said.

"You just drop us and go on to Man Land," Lily said, using her term for Home Depot. "You always like to go there. Pick us up in a couple hours."

Gina Lola turned her head back to Bear's court as he continued. "We just want to go out to the woods, Sam. We can't get all the way to the county park in Bull. But we can take it on a trail from there."

"Yes. We'd like to remember how it used to feel back when we could hike." Lily tried a sad little blink, but she didn't have a lot of eyelashes left, nor false ones like Eunice. She figured she might just look as if she had sand in her eyes.

"Enjoy the woods, fresh air, autumn leaves. Not a problem to walk for most guys. But for me? I need a ride."

Lily wondered if Bear felt a slight stab of shame at that. But she need not have worried. Sam wasn't fooled. "Now that really is the bear shitting in the woods, you old liar. You're going after that little girl. Solana's sister. At that homeless camp."

Bear and Lily looked at each other. Gina Lola looked from one to the next. Finally, Bear confessed. "You're right. You know more about that than we thought, Sam."

"Yes," Lily sounded contrite. Maybe the truth was the way to go here.

Bear confessed. "Didn't want to tell you because we wanted to leave you deniability with Jessica. Didn't want you catching hell."

Sam must have felt his manhood was at stake. "I make my own decisions, damn it all. Always have. Why don't I just go get the kid and leave you two posers out of it?"

"'Cause last thing I knew, you weren't a goddamn woman," Bear snapped. "That child Rosie wouldn't go anywhere with a man, especially an ugly old cowpoke like you."

"But she may listen to me, especially with a note from Solana," Lily the Peacemaker said.

"I'd prefer to send Chrissie because she could just walk it. But she's working today. We can't wait. I'll just have to put up with Lily the Lip."

"Now *that* was snarky," Lily the Lip shot back. "You'll pay for it. Some day. Some how."

Sam snorted a laugh at that threat. Then he shrugged, tapped crap off his pitch fork and returned the tool to the tack area. He loaded Gina Lola into her stall and gave her a lopsided gravenstein apple, plucked from the ranch's own tree. Petting her nose, he mumbled, "Never could leave a lady in distress, could I old girl?"

Without another word to the humans, Sam hitched the flat-bed to his Silverado, loaded Sitting Bull up its ramp, helped Lily and Bear onto the bench seat beside him, and took off for the county park.

✦ ✦ ✦

"Where is the little bitch?" The boss snarled at Joey the Ape.

"I fuckin' swear, boss, I don't know."

"Then grab the sister, you idiot. They'll be getting messages to each other. Girls are like that. We gotta stop it."

"I'm on it. We'll get her."

"You better. Or you're gonna be featured in a film of your own. Something called Road Kill."

✦ ✦ ✦

Bear maneuvered Sitting Bull up the faint path that wound its way from the county park to the homeless camp. The trail was not marked for public access and had never been cleared by forest rangers. It was an unofficial track, created only by the feet of the homeless and maybe deer or elk before them. Overgrowth could easily have hidden a cougar or a Sasquatch. But now a fat-assed shiny red golf cart shoved its way through maple vines and cedar boughs.

Sam hadn't said much at the county park. He'd just squared his jaw and frowned when Bear had him drop them in the parking lot, as close as possible to what passed for the trail head. His only words were, "I'll be back for you in an hour. I'll wait a half hour more. Then I'm coming after you. With Winnie." Winnie was Sam's name for his old Winchester rifle. At the moment, it was secure in his diamond plate truck bed tool box, the one with the auto-lift, gas powered shocks for an easy open lid and the top grade dual lock handles. Nobody would be stealing Winnie any time soon. In fact, the box was Sam's favorite all time purchase from Man Land.

After Bear and Lily left the lot and began negotiating the Bull through the overgrowth, Lily asked, "Why does Sam have that gun with him? He didn't used to carry it."

"Carries it most the time now. In case he ever gets a chance to shoot one of those dogs that attacked Latin Dancer."

"Shoot another dog? After killing one that night?" Lily shook her head. "Sam's not the kind of guy to draw blood just for sport."

"He's pretty sure the pack alpha was rabid. If so, it probably didn't last long, but others will be rabid now, too. Sam thinks they're the real danger to livestock. Besides, he'll never forget the way that colt screamed that night."

"No. I imagine that haunts him." Lily ducked a broken hemlock limb that snapped back as Sitting Bull pushed its way down the narrow trail. She shivered slightly.

"You cold?" Bear asked.

"No. But ...you feel like we're being watched? From just behind the trees?"

She seemed jumpy to Bear, slapping at forest crawlies, real or imagined. "Watched? Could be. We're disturbing the peace of the forest critters."

"Maybe it's that Ape guy, come to collect another trophy from the camp."

Bear made the noise he used for disgust. It sounded like a road grader on gravel.

By the time the trail widened and they burst into a meadow, everyone in the homeless camp knew they were coming. Maybe twenty people of all ages, kids to grammas, stopped whatever they were doing to stare at two septuagenarians in a golf cart.

"Guess we didn't sneak up stealthy as Davy Crockett." Lily dismounted and balanced on her one foot, brushing plant litter off her arms. She gingerly removed a stink bug that had hitched a ride.

The two interlopers looked around the meadow at the canvas village erected there. Nearly a dozen tents stood on wooden planks or pallets that helped keep them dry. A broken-down picnic table was jury-rigged at the hub of the village. Around it, three people prepared food stuffs. Two of them chopped vegetables while a third stirred one of the large pots bubbling away on a battered grill. Then she lifted the lid from another hanging over an open fire. Pleasant odors wafted across the meadow to welcome Bear and Lily, but other than that first glance at them, the people went about their business. Nobody came forward, nobody greeted them.

"Aren't they curious about us?" Lily said to Bear.

"I suspect people in these camps learn to keep their distance from unannounced strangers."

Bear and Lily heard giggles then noticed several children playing tag in front of a vegetable garden cleared on the north end of the meadow. Lily said in a low voice, "Squash vines, corn stalks and the last of the season's tomatoes. These people have been here a long time. Long enough to plant and harvest."

A young teenager was keeping an eye on the kids. She looked like the photo that Solana had given Bear, but the photo wouldn't have been necessary. Rosie was the spitting image of her older sister. Both were small framed. Freckles sprinkled their faces and their hair was the same dark tone of raw honey. Bear thought they were more interesting-looking than pretty.

"Go talk to her, Lily. I'll make friends with the others."

Lily got her walker out of Sitting Bull and picked her way through meadow undergrowth toward Rosie. The girl watched every step, her body as taut and ready to run as a fawn. Maybe her duty to the children held her in check. From the distance of a car length, Lily held out the note. "Hello, Rosie. This is from your sister," she said loud and clear.

"Solana?" Rosie gasped. "She's alive?"

"Alive and safe."

Rosie started to cry. She approached Lily, then backed off, approached again. She finally drew near enough to snatch the note, like a wild thing taking a treat from a human hand. Lily figured that's exactly what she was. She was close enough now to see the wind burns on Rosie's skin and the stringy muscles in her thin arms. She didn't smell bad, but she looked dingy. This kid had been living rough for many weeks.

Rosie unfolded the note and read. When she finished, she looked up at Lily. Her face was aglow with joy.

Lily smiled. "My name is Lily. We're here to take you to Solana."

Rosie said, "Watch the children for just a sec." Then she ran to one of the tents, stopped briefly to add, "Please," and ducked inside.

Meanwhile, Bear approached the ancient picnic table. A rawboned woman finally stopped stirring one of the pots and eyed him. She was middle-aged, maybe in her fifties, dressed in a mismatched grab bag of clothing. Nonetheless, she had a confident stance with the unmistakable aura of authority. Bear felt this woman had been a boss. Or maybe a matriarch before finding her way downhill to a camp like this.

Her strong, self-assured voice matched the image. "I'm Rita, the Tent Master. My job is to make sure all is in order. May I ask your business here?"

"I'm Alvin 'Bear' Jacobs. We've come with a message for Rosie."

"I can see that." The woman watched Rosie disappear into the tent. "But a message from whom?"

"Her sister, Solana."

Rita's stern face softened. "Oh, we've worried about Solana. Is she okay?"

"She's had a hard time. But she's safe now." Bear told Rita enough of Solana's story for her to accept the truth of what he was saying.

"If Rosie goes with you, can you help these sisters?" Hope added a glint of pleasure to the haggard eyes.

"That's why Lily and I are here." He indicated his old friend who had picked a wildflower that looked like a big fuzzy raspberry. She was telling the children who now surrounded her, "It's called rosy spirea. Rosy. Just like your friend."

Rita stiffened. "You're not ATF? Or Child Support?"

"No, nothing like that. Just a friend to Solana."

"Of course you are," Rita said with obvious skepticism.

"Look at me, Rita. I'm way too old for sirens and mars lights and packing heat. I'm a PI, retired long ago."

She stared longer and he was quiet. She was making her decision and he gave her room. In their silence with each other, he heard a child ask, "What's this blue one?" and Lily answer, "A gentian. Its cup closes when it rains to protect the pollen."

"We've had troubles with lawmen before. Or people who say they're lawmen." Rita frowned, but then her posture relaxed. She began stirring again. Bear remained quiet, but understood that she'd decided to trust him. "Our camp is not sanctioned, of course, even here on national park land. Sometimes people hassle us. A couple men came through just the night before Solana disappeared."

"Have you lost people before?"

Rita gave him a weary smile. "People disappear from homeless camps all the time. Usually because they want to. Not always. The rangers mostly leave us alone, but they're not the only ones in this forest. We don't draw attention to ourselves or do anything to make authorities move us on."

"Oh? How do you manage that?" Bear tried to keep skepticism out of his voice.

"Self-regulation. We each have jobs. There's a Donations Coordinator and an Arbitrator and everyone serves security watch schedules. We tolerate no violence, no illegal substances, no theft, no convictions for sex offenses, and no shirking of work details. We're probably better managed than the town where you live." Her weary eyes telegraphed a clear invitation to verbal battle.

Bear was impressed. He could see that dignity was part of the human condition, even here.

As he and Rita talked, Bear watched Rosie leave the tent with two back-packs that appeared stuffed full. She went to the other people at the table and hugged each. One of them went to watch the children so Lily, breath-ing heavily from the effort, rejoined Bear. Softly Rosie said, "We can go now." She indicated one of the backpacks. "This one is Solana's stuff."

Rita thanked Bear. She told Rosie to be careful and to listen to Solana. They hugged goodbye. The whole encounter had taken no more than ten minutes.

As they motored back down the path, Rosie bounced in the back seat. She giggled at the absurdity of Sitting Bull, and she reached up to shove branches out of the way. But she wasn't really happy. If anything, Bear and Lily could feel her tension increase the further they whirred along.

Finally, she blurted, "We should hurry. They won't stay quiet."

"The people in the camp? Don't you trust them?" Bear wanted to be-lieve the group would protect her.

"They'll tell the others. The ones out fishing or gathering blackberries. And who they'll tell, well, Solana is the only person on earth I really trust."

As if on cue, Lily said, "Do you hear that rustling? Behind us?"

"Probably just the wind coming up," Bear said.

"Can we hurry?"

"It ain't a Mazerati," Bear grumped, but he pushed Sitting Bull as hard as he could. When they putted back into the county park, Sam was there, leaning against the Silverado's nose. Bear figured he'd never really left.

Bear and Lily introduced Rosie to Sam, and he evoked another giggle when he tipped his cowboy hat at her and called her 'Miss." Bear supposed they were a funny trio when assessed by a fifteen year old.

Sam loaded Rosie's back packs into the cab's back seat and she clam-bered in beside them. The three adults took their stations in the front, Lily sandwiched between Sam and Bear. As they left the park, Lily whispered to Bear, "Just so you know, I never really lost the feeling of being watched."

"Yep," he replied. "You managed to pass it on to me."

✦ ✦ ✦

Sam delivered his passengers to Latin's Ranch then headed off to the barn. Over his shoulder he shot back at them, "My part in this is done. Jessica asks? I've been cleaning horse shit all day."

"Pay no attention to Sam, dear," Lily said to Rosie. "He's very glad you're safe now. We all are. Just go knock on that door." She pointed to the trailer.

"But what is this place?" Rosie asked. Lily followed the girl's sightline from the horse barn on her left to the old house on her right where Eunice, Charlie and Frankie were on the porch watching them. Even Rachael came out the front door to watch, although it was Eunice who was holding BB.

"This is where we live, Rosie. You might say we were all homeless, too, until we found each other. Now go see your sister. She's in the trailer. She'll tell you all about it."

At that moment, Solana came bursting out. "Rosie!" she cried.

The two girls grabbed each other, squealing in voices pitched high as dolphins and delivered at warp speed.

Lily and Bear looked on. "What language is that?" he asked.

"Teenage girl," Lily answered.

"Hurts my ears. Let me see if I can cut in." Bear harrumphed. Once, twice. "HARRUMPH!"

The sisters stopped their celebration and stared at him. Bear gave them orders to stay out of sight and out of trouble in the trailer for the rest of the day. They nodded at him. He trusted them as much as he'd trust feral kittens left on their own. But he couldn't keep them if they didn't want to stay. The best he could do was to suggest Lily stay with them for a while.

Of course, that pissed her off as if she were a third feral cat. "You're not dumping me, big man," she whispered to him. I'll see if Rachael would like to spend some time with them. She'd probably enjoy other young people for a while."

"Especially if she can get them to take care of Baby Boy."

"Whatever works. Okay, what's next?"

"Time to involve Cupcake."

✦   ✦   ✦

A 1996 Chevy Caprice pulled in the drive and rumbled its way to a stop in front of Latin's Ranch. Bear knew it was a wolf in sheep's clothing, that there was serious muscle under that Sunday-driver exterior. It had been a cop cruiser, a V8 Supersport, back in the day when the good guys could outrun the bad. It wasn't in mint condition but it was no beater, either. The land yacht was now painted a deep blueberry that sparkled in those rare moments when the Pacific Northwest sun chose to shine.

Deputy Detective Josephine Keegan of the Major Crimes Unit stepped out of the unmarked vehicle. Seeing her in Reeboks, jeans and a Copper River Salmon t-shirt, Bear thought she looked prettier than in her sheriff's uniform or even her business casual plain clothes. Her dark curls bounced merrily, free of the knot that usually trapped them behind her head.

"Bear. Lily," Keegan said, approaching them where they sat in wicker porch chairs waiting for her. It was early afternoon, and the autumn breeze would soon chase them indoors.

"Cupcake," said Bear voicing the nickname he had used years ago when he was a PI in his prime and Jo Keegan was a rookie with the sheriffs department.

"Detective Keegan," said Lily.

Keegan joined them on the porch and sat legs akimbo on one of the redwood benches in order to face them. "You called me here on a much deserved day off. I was about to change Big Blue's plugs and air filter. What's up?"

"Need you to do something," Bear said.

"We could use your help with a serious problem," Lily the Diplomat said.

Keegan sighed. "Why do I think this is gonna screw up my day?"

Bear and Lily proceeded to tell Jo about Solana's kidnapping, Rosie's rescue and the rest of their fears. While they talked, Bear watched Keegan's body change. She uncrossed her legs, straightened her back, tightened her muscles. The cop was on point. She finally broke into his monologue. "So where are these girls?"

"They're safe. Tucked away."

"I want to talk to them."

"They don't want to talk to you." Bear sat back, crossed his arms over the expanse of his plaid-flannelled chest.

"That's bullshit," Keegan answered, her eyebrows knitted together in a frown.

The Diplomat stilled the waters. "Detective, they're scared. Homeless kids and cops don't always mix or so I understand. I'm sure they'll come around in time." Lily smiled.

Keegan's frown continued but she let it pass. "Snuff films. You're kidding, right? Shit, that goes back to before I joined the department. Haven't heard of them in years."

"They're back. Maybe in an even worse form."

"How do you know?"

"Can't tell you." Bear had to minimize Frankie's involvement. "At least not yet. Too many suppositions and too few facts to take the story to the authorities officially. That's why we're talking unofficially."

"Yeah, well, maybe you should wait 'til you get your story straight."

"Detective," Bear growled. "People are being kidnapped. They're forced to appear in snuff films. And they are dying. I'm sure of it."

Keegan disengaged from the fight. She looked sad to Bear. A detective's life is one sad thing after another. He knew that from his own career, a career that had nearly broken him.

He didn't back off and pressed his advantage. "I can't prove it yet. That's where you and your partner come in. *You* can stop it."

"Okay. But just what exactly do you want from us, keeping in mind that my partner thinks you are a meddling snoop, and I am inclined to agree most of the time?"

Bear gave Keegan an overview of his plan. When he finished he said, "You've worked with my hunches before, and I haven't led you wrong."

"True enough," Keegan said. "But this will be too much for Clay."

"It's too much to ask him to save lives?"

"Oh, horseshit. You know that's not what I mean. But he's gonna think this sounds crazy even by your standards."

Lily intervened. "Yes, it does sound crazy, Detective Keegan. Jo. But I believe it's true. So do Charlie and Eunice. And you know we're not just brainless old has-beens. You need to listen to Bear about this."

You go, Lily. Lay it on thick. Bear was damn proud of his protégé until she went a bit too far.

"This time he's not just poking his nose where it doesn't belong."

"Hey, wait a minute ..."

But Lily continued. "If you and Clay would listen to him together, I think he can convince you both that something is very wrong."

"I don't know, Lily," Keegan snorted a derisive laugh. "My partner says Bear's more hindrance than help."

"I thought he might be interested in breaking up a ring of slime balls," Bear snarled.

"Yeah, yeah. I'll talk to him. But Clay will take a lot of convincing."

"That young man needs to unclench his butt just a bit, don't you think?" Lily asked, dropping her sweetie-pie role. Bear knew her loyalty to him ran high even though she was half in lust with Keegan's handsome young partner, Clay Galligan. All the ladies at Latin's Ranch were. Bear had overheard them discussing Galligan's ass in terms of prime beef.

Keegan bristled some at Lily's comment. "I know he might strike you as, ah, uptight. Too by-the-book. But he's a really smart cop. We've worked together since he joined up. I'm lucky he's happy with a female partner since not all the guys feel that way. That's made things a damn sight easier on me than it used to be when the person next to me was hostile. I trust him, Lily. Even if he doesn't care for the intervention of those he considers outsiders."

Now it was Bear's turn as the diplomat. "We get that, Keegan. But this is important. Can you get him here for a meeting tonight?"

"Uh, sure. Like that's gonna be easy."

"Should be."

"Oh? Why's that?"

"It's Sicilian night."

Keegan stood to go. "No problem. We'll both be here."

"Thought so."

"One more thing, Bear."

"Yeah?"

"Don't call me Cupcake."

CHAPTER SIX

Case Notes
September 18, 9 p.m.

It happens once a month. We call it Sicilian Night.
Frankie, in addition to his life as a low life, is an amateur chef. The tastes of the Mediterranean are deep in his DNA. Through nothing but charm and iron will, he's managed to teach our fiery Mexican cook Aurora a few culinary tricks. Together, they come up with hybrid recipes I call Mexicilian.
Theirs isn't always a happy collaboration. They bicker for hours in the kitchen all through the day before Sicilian Night. When Bear and I sit on the back patio, sharing the Seattle Times, *we often hear their squalls. Should oregano be the astringent, spicy Mexican variety or the less bitter species from Italy? Does the sweet, nutty flavor of the Mexican Manzanilla olive deliver a finer oil than the saltier Sicilian Castelvetrano? Should a nation that fries ice cream consider itself an equal to one that invented gelato?*
Today's spat was about wine.
"Tonight we serve a Mexican cabernet from the Valle de Guadalupe," Aurora announced.
"A country known for tequila knows niente *of grapes," Frankie countered.*
"A man from an island that uses grape seeds for liquor talks to me about the grape? My Mexico has made wines since the sixteenth century."

"So new? My country has made wine for much more time."

"Okay then. You don't drink tonight with the rest of us."

I think maybe Aurora won this round.

Anyhoo. About Deputy Clay Galligan. All Irish blue eyes, dark curls, tight butt, six-foot-something of him. The women here have each been crushing on him in our own ways, but it's Aurora who fell like a soufflé. When she knows Clay is coming for dinner, she nearly drifts through the air, her feet never touching the ground. She forgets she's married. She forgets she's older than his mother. Her cooking escalates to ambrosia-from-the-gods status.

For his part, I imagine Clay rarely has a good meal. We're talking bachelor cop here. Probably a cheeseburger is as high on the food chain as he gets day to day. So the first time he experienced Sicilian Night, it was as though the heavens parted.

Nothing about Bear or me could get him here. We're just old butt-inskies. But tell Clay it's Sicilian night? The sneer disappears. Those eyes sparkle like a tropical ocean. A heart wrecking grin lights up his face. And we all get the hell out of the way between him and the dining room table.

- Lily Gilbert, Amused Assistant to PI Bear Jacobs

Since the cops were coming to Sicilian night, the sisters chose to stay hidden in the trailer. Lily had Chrissie make a pizza run for them – behind Aurora's back, of course – and also deliver DVDs that young girls might like. In other words, Sam's John Wayne collection would stay on the shelf that night.

In the dining room, all the residents wore their dearest finery, the silks, gems and jackets from days gone by when eating out was a special occasion. Tonight's entree was something Aurora dubbed Sicilicana Surprise, a slow baked mélange of shredded beef, Italian parsley, basil, homemade noodles, queso fresco and parmesan served bubbling hot with slices of lemon and hunks of crusty garlic bread. Those who could have wine shared the Mexican cabernet, but Aurora also served a peace offering of Sicilian grappa with dessert.

The dinner party was large and raucous. All the regulars were there: the residents, Jessica, Ben and Sylvia. Guests tonight included Vinny in a million dollar suit and Sam wearing his newest, fresh brushed Stetson. Even the two detectives had upgraded plain clothes to fairly fancy clothes. Clay's leather jacket fit his triangular upper body like a kid glove. Lily whispered to Eunice, "How can a guy built like that sit on such a small butt without tipping over?"

Ben's daughter, Rachael, appeared midway through the meal, with BB in tow. Once she met the godlike Clay, she dumped the baby on Bear's lap, grabbed a kitchen chair and forced it between the two deputies. She licked her lips and flipped her hair at Clay until she discovered he was law enforcement, then she reverted to her customary sullen mope.

Aurora would not be so easily deterred. "Another serving, Señor Sheriff? You must keep up your strength to defend me." Bat, bat.

By the end of the meal, Bear added blush red to the Irish cop's list of colorful attributes like black curls and glacial blue eyes. And if he wasn't such a trained investigator, Bear might have missed the subtle eye game going on between Sylvia and Vinny. He wondered if Lily had noticed that particular thriller unfold.

✦ ✦ ✦

Oh, dear.

Lily had always thought her daughter was a little too structured. She'd worried that Sylvia, married to a conservative gay man, had missed out on life's most sensuous passions. But when Kyle died, Lily had to admit she'd been wrong, that Sylvia had been fulfilled by the love between them and was inconsolable without him.

Lily had watched from the sidelines as Sylvia's bond with Tony solidified. He was not only Kyle's former lover but also Frankie Sapienza's grandson. Lily worried he would hurt her daughter again when all was said and done. But she'd been wrong about that, too. Tony and Sylvia had been shattered together and walked out of that valley of darkness together.

If Sylvia had been patched together again, it was in no small part from sharing Tony's love of Kyle.

Still and all, Sylvia lived a quiet, contained life. She took no chances, and Lily wished she'd spread her wings a little. She wanted her daughter to experience life's smorgasbord the way she herself had. Having a variety of passionate, wild stories in her memory bank was the currency Lily lived on in her old age.

But, for the love of God, was it possible her meticulous, uptight daughter was going too far? Lily had seen the eye play. Might Sylvia actually be falling for a *mobster*? Was she spreading her wings so wide she'd fly straight into the sun?

Lily got along with Vinny well enough, but she understood the importance of his stature in *La Famiglia*. She'd seen the whole Godfather series, and she knew things didn't go all that well for Diane Keaton. But was it any of her business? Didn't she owe her daughter the freedom of choice that she demanded Sylvia allow her? Her own words about autonomy were biting her in the butt big time.

Oh dear. What to do. Oh dear.

All this was bubbling away in Lily's brain when the diners found other places to be after dinner. Only Bear and she stayed at the table with the two deputy sheriffs.

✦   ✦   ✦

Jo Keegan had already briefed her partner on their conversation from earlier in the day. Bear didn't bother trying to convince Clay that he was right about a group creating snuff films. Instead, he appealed to the cop's vanity.

"I can't do this without you," Bear said. "The role as I see it calls for a young man, strong, smart. Someone who can pass as a downsized executive."

Clay didn't exactly melt like putty at the idea, but full of Mexicilian food and wine, he at least listened while Bear went over the plan to send him in undercover as a newly homeless man.

"You've lost a corporate job," Bear said developing a cover story, "and not found another in the flooded Seattle market. So you've come north of the city hoping to find something in this area. That explains why you're not known in the local shelters and food banks. The fact that you're obviously in good shape, probably from workouts in the gym with the other execs, shouldn't make people suspicious since you're recently homeless."

"So you think I'll find someone at the camp who knows about the movie making," Clay said.

Bear shrugged. "Maybe. One of them may be a snitch. Or something worse. There's what may be a suspicious sounding lawman or two coming around. They were there right before Solana disappeared. Maybe an ATF agent, maybe a city cop. Could be others."

"Why do you think they're cops?"

Because Frankie says so, goddammit. The mobster knows the mobs have infiltrated your ranks.

Bear could not say it without involving the Sapienza family, and he'd promised he would not name them. He tried for other reasons to convince the deputy sheriffs that there may be a bad apple in the law enforcement barrel. "Well, first, because the woman who runs the homeless camp thinks one may be. And second, ah ... it makes sense a cop close to the street knows where to find victims that wouldn't be missed." It sounded weak even to Bear.

"No other reason?" Clay glowered.

"Nothing I can share." Bear glowered back.

Finally, Keegan said, "Clay and I have talked, Bear. And we'll go along with you for a while at least. But we've changed your plan."

Bear managed to stifle a growl. "Yeah? How?"

Lily the Peacemaker chimed in. "Isn't it just wonderful how one idea can plus another?"

"We'll do it. But I go undercover, not Clay."

Bear sat, stunned. He didn't want that. He was fond of Cupcake. And more worried about her safety than Galligan's. But he could never say it. Keegan would bust his chops for not treating her as an equal for any job, dangerous or otherwise. Since he couldn't fess up, he continued to shut up.

"Clay's a great cop but a lousy actor," Keegan explained. "Undercover work is not his forte."

"Hate to admit it, but it's true. The department doesn't let me do it anymore. Say I'm a liability," Clay conceded. Bear thought he saw another blush on the kid's cheeks, this one not from Aurora's overzealous nurturing.

"But if anyone can play a broken down executive, it's me. I love that shit." Keegan's bright smile targeted Bear, but still he maintained his silence. "Or maybe I'll be a runaway wife. Whatever, if I see something suspicious, I'll get in touch right away. If other officers are involved, they're more likely to be rangers than sheriffs. I won't be recognized. If I am, I am. If my cover's blown, then we'll work out another way."

"She'll do the job perfect," Clay interrupted, "and I'll tell Delacruz what we're up to."

Lily looked puzzled. "Why not keep it secret even from your boss if you don't know who is involved?"

"We can't take on other government agencies without his support, Lily. And we'll get it," Keegan answered.

Clay added, "Any local cop wants to show up a fed if one is involved, especially when the local is a professional brown nose like Sheriff J. L. Delacruz."

✦   ✦   ✦

Sylvia kissed her mother good-bye. It was immediately after dessert on Sicilian night because Lily had hurried her out the door.

"I have an important meeting to attend," the near-octogenarian said.

Just great. Even my old mother has more of a social life than I do.

Sylvia was feeling petulant as she crunched across the gravel drive toward her car, digging in her Coach bag for her keys. Somehow she'd allowed Vinny to escape without as much as saying good night. Her skills were rusty, not that they'd ever been very damned good. If Bear had been walking beside her, she would have asked him to hum *What Kind of Fool Am I?*

"Good evening, *Signora* Henderson."

Her leap was as spectacular as that of a gazelle. "Oh, ah, hi. Please, call me Sylvia." The deep, sensuous voice had startled her out of her reverie about the very man who owned it.

Sylvia had dropped her keys and bent to retrieve them, but Vinny beat her to it. He even unlocked her car with the key fob and opened the door for her. "I see you at the movie before. When I am with my nephews."

"Oh? Really? Well then," she blathered as she tried to slide gracefully into the Lexus. She nearly made it until she caught a heel on the door-frame and her shoe clattered to the ground.

"Permit me," Vinny said as he picked up the shoe to place it back on her foot.

Are my feet smelly? Is there a run in my nylon? Oh God, I need a pedicure.

"Gosh, thanks," Sylvia managed as his hand on her ankle sent signals all the way to the other end of her leg.

Did I really just say Gosh?

Vinny straightened. "I did not see that you were with a man at the movie."

"Oh no, I was alone. No, not alone. I mean I was with a girlfriend. A whole bunch of girlfriends. You know, girl's night out."

Jesus. Shut the hell up.

"Possibly you would consider attending a movie with me? When your girlfriends can spare you."

"Of course, I mean I would certainly consider it were you to ask me."

"Then I shall make a plan."

As Vinny's smile revealed his beautiful white teeth, all Sylvia could say was, "Uh-huh."

"Good night for now. And drive with much care." He touched her cheek just before he closed her car door.

Make a plan? How about leaping into the back seat with me?

"Good night then," she managed to say. "I'll look forward to it."

When she got home, Sylvia sat on the side of her bed and picked up the nightstand photo of her dead husband. She stared at his intelligent, slender face so dissimilar from the sharp planes and piercing eyes of Vinny.

"Well, Kyle," she finally asked the photo. "Is this how you felt about Tony? Something so breathlessly ... *different*? Do I have the courage to fol-low my heart the way you did?"

She stood, removed her make-up, added a night cream that promised miracles, and changed into a light cotton nightgown after neatly folding her sweater and hanging her dress. In the end, she had to admit to the truth. Kyle could have lost everything by following his heart. She herself had nothing to lose.

She took one last look at Kyle before turning out the nightstand light. "I'd like to try, my love. I'll try."

✦ ✦ ✦

Much later that night, Jessica and Ben rested in the bed intertwined and sweating. Jessica's leg, trapped between Ben's had lost most of its feeling. "Let go," she muttered.

"I don't think I can do that again for a while, Babe," he muttered back.

She chuckled. "I mean let go of my leg."

"Oh." He lifted and rolled, releasing her. Needles worked their way down to her foot as blood rushed back in. She rolled, too, spooning against him. Soon his breathing took on the steady rhythm of sleep.

Jessica stayed awake. For a while she listened for activity in the rooms below, but everything seemed still other than a distant TV and air moving in the heat ducts. Latin's Ranch was settled for the night. Her wards were all safe. The quiet was luxurious. She began to doze.

The baby's sudden cry shattered the peace. Ben sat up, put on pajama bottoms and headed down the stairs to the room that Rachael shared with her son. Jessica knew Ben would feed the baby and probably hand him over to one of the willing seniors who would rock away BB's insomnia as well as his or her own.

Ben never asked Jessica to help, and she never explained why she didn't. She figured that he assumed she needed her sleep to run her business with the constant attentiveness it demanded. That was true enough. But it wasn't her real reason.

Jessica rolled onto her back and spread an arm out over the part of the bed that was still warm from his body. She hoped his heart would make it through the beating it would no doubt take from Rachael. Jessica had no trust in the girl's ability to cowgirl up to motherhood. The baby was just another burden to the street addict.

If she could just take the baby away from Rachael and raise him with Ben as their own, Jessica would be deliriously happy. As it was, she had to stay away to protect her own heart. And to give Ben time to figure out what he would do when he had to chose between the wellbeing of BB, his daughter and Jessica. Door Number One, Two or Three. He had huge decisions ahead, and she needed to stay out of the way to let him make them. She would not pressure him with her needs, not now.

After the death of her husband, Ben had been there, cared for her, supported her until she could see him for the strong, gentle man he was. She needed to have the same patience with him. A tear rolled down her cheek and hit the pillow.

Please, Ben. If you can, make what's best for you what's best for me, too.

CHAPTER SEVEN

Case Notes
September 19, 10 am

Everyone is busy this morning. Jessica and Ben took two of the hay-
burners up to the Cascades for a two-day trail ride. Wonder what
will get sorer ... their butts from the saddles or their backs from sleep-
ing on the ground. Ben's colt, Latin Dancer, is too scarred from that
dog attack to be handsome, but they tell me he's recovering enough
confidence to do well on the trails. Jessica says Ben is gentle with the
horse, helping him regain self-assurance after such a disastrous strike.
If you ask me, Ben has been pretty damn gentle with Jessica, too,
helping her regain self-assurance after the death of her husband. I
swear, if the two of them don't commit soon, I may grab them both by
the hair and knock noggins. Not that I believe marriage is the only
happy ending to a romance. Far from it. But in this case? I worry
about Rachael's ability, or desire, to raise Baby Boy. It couldn't hurt
for him to have legally bound grandparents ready to step in if need
be. Not my business, I know. I'm just saying.
Aurora is showing the two sisters where to gather blackberries in Jes-
sica's pastures along the tree line. Mexican blackberry tart tonight.
She makes it with mascarpone and a touch of lime. Yum. Bear fussed
about the girls being outdoors, but he can't expect Solana and Rosie
to stay in that trailer forever. They're bored and eager to help out.
They promised not to wander.

Sometime today, Detective Keegan will be hiking to the homeless camp to start the undercover investigation. I know Bear is upset by that. It was his plan, sure. But he hates putting others in danger with his schemes, even though Keegan is a smart, experienced cop who may be one of the scariest things in the woods when she's riled. No matter how much I might argue that the decision is hers, Bear would argue that he put her in the position to make the decision. So yes, if you look at it that way, I guess we all carry responsibility for each other one way or another.

Clay is being a butt. A mighty fine butt but a butt nonetheless. Now that Bear has written a note to Rita the Tent Master introducing Keegan, Clay has as much as told him to keep his snout out of things. Like that's going to happen.

Anyhoo. The five of us residents are about to leave for our senior center date. Rachael will have to take care of BB on her own for a few hours. I imagine that explains her frownie face. I suppose I should offer to stay and help. But today I have other fish to fry. I have a secret. Don't want to get Sylvia's or Jessica's hopes up. Mine either, for that matter. But I'm stronger now. More fit, mind and body. I think I just may walk again.

- Lily Gilbert, Two-Stepping Assistant to PI Bear Jacobs

Jo Keegan was a tough, self-possessed officer of the law. In her time, she'd seen plenty of mayhem that would scare most people so straight they'd never bend again. There was just one fear she kept on the hush hush, a fear virtually unheard of in the Pacific Northwest: she hated hiking in the woods.

When she was a child, she'd walked smack into a branch swarming with a hatching of baby spiders. They crawled all over her cheek as she frantically tried to wipe them away. Next, they infested her hands. She'd never forgotten the incident. As an adult officer of the law, nothing terrified her the way a spider did. She lived in dread that her fellow officers, most of them males, would find out. They'd stock her desk with rubber tarantulas or dangle black widow lookalikes from her prowl car's mirrors. The bastards would be merciless from here to eternity. She wished her partner Clay was with her to clear the path. But she was equally glad he was nowhere around to laugh at her fears.

It was two days since Sicilian Night. It had taken that long for her to push her other cases aside and for Clay to report he'd convinced Sheriff Delacruz to go along with the plan. Keegan was now armed with a backpack and wardrobe she'd picked up at Value Village. Clean, serviceable but obviously used. She'd run a check on Rita's background, found no reason not to follow Bear's instinct that the woman was dependable. She carried a note from Bear to Rita that explained what she was doing there, and she had a prepaid cell phone to give the Tent Master. Rita could call Bear or Clay for confirmation if she felt the need.

Keegan's only form of ID was a false driver's license. The detectives kept a few on hand for undercover work. This one was in the bullshit name of Caliente Desiree, and the photo looked vaguely like her if she had gone in for circus make-up. Keegan figured she knew exactly what sort of undercover assignments it had served before.

Her plan was to stay in the homeless camp for a few days, up to a week. She'd ferret out a camp member who was fingering victims for the snuff films, if such a person existed. Or she'd be there if a faux lawman showed. Or the guy Solana called the Ape. Once she found a suspicious character, she'd call Clay for back-up.

She didn't really need him, of course. She could take down any number of bad guys herself. But if he'd take on the eight-leggers, she'd be glad to have him around.

✦ ✦ ✦

On Friday and Saturday afternoons, Vinny drove the five residents to a community senior center. All costs at the center were paid for by Sylvia, to give them time to socialize with others, and also to give Jessica time off. This wasn't just out of compassion. Neither Sylvia nor the people who lived at Latin's Ranch could afford for the caregiver to burn out. Jessica was their guardian angel, virtually impossible to ever replace.

"Keegan should be getting to the homeless camp about now," Bear said to Lily. They were in the front seat of the Caddy, with Eunice, Charlie and Frankie in the back.

Lily, tucked between Vinny and Bear, felt like a thin slice of pastrami in a Kaiser roll. She wriggled for more room, elbowing Bear in his ample waist. She didn't touch Vinny just in case she set off some weapon of mass destruction.

"I'm worried for her," Lily said. Jo Keegan was Bear's connection but had become important to them all. A friendship was even growing between the lady cop and Jessica.

"Don't be. She's a tough cookie."

"Don't you mean a tough cupcake?"

Bear raised a lip in what passed for a grin.

"Besides," Lily continued. "Today, I have my own outing to worry about."

"Sure you don't want me to go with you?"

"Don't think so. They really hated you there, Bear. Chrissie is taking me."

Chrissie Metzger, off duty that day, was nevertheless at the senior center to meet Lily when Vinny dropped them off. As the others entered the front door to find the Wii console or the bridge tournament or the pickle ball court, each had a word with Lily.

"Give 'em hell, old girl," Charlie squeaked with a snappy salute.

"You can do this," Eunice said with a hug that tinkled her bangles together. "You can do anything, Lily."

Frankie bowed and kissed her hand. "*In bocca al lupo!* I wish you luck, *cara mia.*"

Bear whispered words so low Lily figured that no one else heard. But they all would see the tears in her eyes if they cared to look. It was rare for the big man to say anything so sweet.

Chrissie helped Lily transfer from her wheelchair to the passenger seat of her boyfriend Will's bilious green Hyundai, and off they went. She was the only Latin's Ranch nursing aide who knew Lily's plan. Her complicity with it was imperative. Chrissie had quite literally kept Lily alive for years.

Lily's amputation occurred after years of struggle with neuropathy, brought on by diabetes. Her nerves were damaged, so her lower extremities were numb. Chrissie's diligence in unwrapping, cleaning and rewrapping the stump was no small part of Lily's return to health. It was her personal mission to keep killer infections at bay. In the deepest of admiration, Lily called the aide her Wrapper Chick.

This wasn't Lily's first visit to *It's Swell to Be Well* geriatric health clinic. In fact, her initial contact had been anything but swell. Bear and she investigated it when they had been on the trail of the body parts trade. Bear bullied the receptionist while Lily put up such a noisy fuss that the doctor finally emerged from the inner sanctum to see what was going on. As it turned out, the clinic had been innocent of any wrong-doing. The same couldn't be said for Bear and Lily who had extracted the information they needed by being real assholes.

Even though that episode was long since locked away in her closed case notes, Lily had always felt bad about frightening Dr. Flannery. She thought she owed him the favor of her business, so she'd made this appointment with him instead of her usual practitioner. Since she was unsure whether the good doctor would feel the same, she hoped he wouldn't recognize her as long as she wasn't with Bear.

If Dr. Flannery recognized her, he gave no sign of it. He was a slender man whose head came to a point above his male pattern baldness. He looked as if he was busting through a fluffy gray cloud.

"Tell me Dr. Flannery, am I too old for a peg leg?" Lily began.

Dr. Flannery smiled then said, "It isn't about age. It's about attitude. Do you think you can wear a prothesis?"

"I think I want to try."

While Chrissie unwrapped the stump, or what the doctor called Lily's residual limb, he said, "Of course it won't be a real peg leg made from a mast. You probably won't get a parrot for your shoulder, either. And you'll have to see yet another specialist if you want a patch for your eye."

Lily felt herself relax in the warmth of his smile. But she was no fool. She knew this would be one of her hardest challenges ever. She'd heard others claim that, what with all the support accessories now available, life in a wheelchair was much easier than the battle with an artificial limb.

But to walk again. Imagine that!

Dr. Flannery examined the residual limb which ended just below Lily's knee. Meanwhile, he asked if she could learn new things, and whether she wanted a prosthesis to move better or look better, and did she recognize the effort it would take physically to master it. Then he questioned Chrissie. "What about you, young lady? Do you think Lily can handle an artificial limb?"

"I think she can handle anything. But there are issues." Chrissie explained Lily's difficulty with skin ulcers and neuropathy, how susceptible she was to infection. She told him about her own vigilance against sores on Lily's aging skin, skin that was thin with no elasticity, skin so delicate a prosthesis could tear it. "I worry about her trying it, doctor. But I guess I worry more about what she'll do if somebody tells her she can't."

Lily snorted in defiance but in truth, she was petrified of being turned down.

When Dr. Flannery was done and Chrissie was wrapping Lily's leg again, he said, "I'm sorry to disappoint you about that heavy wooden peg. But if you'll accept a lightweight plastic and carbon graphite limb with a spring in its step, I believe we can fix you up."

"Really? I mean, really?" Lily felt like a five-year-old meeting Santa. She couldn't wait to tell the others, especially Bear. Now she could not only work with him, but stand tall beside him.

"I'm sending you to a prosthetist who'll fit one just for you, one that Medicare approves. He'll also help you through an amputee rehab program. But, Ms. Gilbert, it won't be easy. If you can't deal with it, I don't want you to plunge into depression. Just how much you'll be able to do, well, time will tell. There are many degrees of success between standing still and running marathons."

"Hell, doc, I won't be any worse off than I am now," she scoffed. But she knew it would be worse. Failure would be proof of her fragility. Proof of decline.

A very cheery Chrissie took Lily back to the senior center to join the others. The aide, sworn to secrecy from the rest of the Latin's Ranch staff, hustled away to spent the remainder of her day off with her kids. As Lily pushed herself into the center to find the others, eager to share her news, she was surprised to see Vinny's long black Cadillac parked in the lot.

Wonder why he's here. It's way too early to pick us up.

✦ ✦ ✦

Bear was about to take one of Frankie's knights. He didn't always beat the old don, but it was their second game today at the senior center, and the earlier win was in his column. He had high hopes for this game, too, as he looked into space for a moment of thought about his sneak attack on the stylized horse head. Suddenly that space was filled with the imposing presence of Vinny Tononi.

Two oldsters at a nearby table decided their game of cribbage could wait for another day. They skittered out of the room, quietly excusing themselves to the looming giant. When they were gone, Vinny bowed to Frankie Sapienza. "So sorry, *Padrone*. I have news."

Ordinarily nobody interrupted Frankie when a game was on the line. Bear either, for that matter. But Vinny was no ordinary interruption. When Frankie looked up at his companion, the old man's fragility disappeared as if by magic. Bear sensed the presence of the hard guy the don had once been.

Frankie commanded, "Inform, *per favore*."

"There ez establishment for the serving of alcohol to law enforcement. A pub run by Irishmen. Life is very low there."

Bear actually laughed. "Yea, called The Abbey. Seedy. It can get pretty wild. At least in the old days." It had been a long time since Bear had participated in pub crawls.

"This ez the place. A dangerous place, I think."

Bear wanted to point out that a cop bar might be particularly dangerous for a mobster, but he decided to let it pass.

"Our man in this place hears something you must know." Vinny addressed the don but glanced toward Bear as well.

"You have a man in a cop bar?" Bear asked.

He wasn't really surprised, but he felt a chill when Frankie looked to him and said, "We have a man in each place of importance."

Of course you do.

Frankie turned back to his bodyguard. "Continue, Vinny."

"He has been there often, ez now what you call regular customer. This time he see bartender slide a small package to man at the bar." Vinny turned to Bear. "Our men who do this job, they know a drop when they see one."

Of course they do.

"Our man gets close to this customer. They drink together. The customer, he becomes indiscreet. Mentions film he ordered and picked up." Vinny lowered his voice. "It is not nice, this DVD he described. A murder. The beating and hanging of a *moulinyan* by men in white robes and hoods. I do not use the word he used. It is an ugly word."

"I think I can guess it." Bear interjected. He remembered 'Black Dude' as described by Solana. Was he the subject of the film that this purchaser described? Bear felt another chill even though he was usually too warm. He hoped Solana would never discover what had become of a man who'd actually tried to help her escape.

"Our man buys this asshole many drinks. Ez easy to keep him talking in a low voice. They are not overheard. He ordered this film because these people are taking his buddies' jobs. Ez to get even, yes? And to share with those friends."

Bear made a noise so disgusted that it was a foul oath all on its own. Then he said, "There's more, and it's worse, right?"

"Si. He say you can order any kind of victim you want. From a place called the Dark Web."

"*Dios mio*," Frankie muttered. "This man, he orders death. Ez not sensible hit on bad guy ... ez contract on innocent. A wrong thing. *Cattivo.* We hear of this before, this bad business. Now we have proof."

Bear nodded, working it through aloud. "If you have enough cash, you have a film made just for you. A suitable candidate is found, dressed up like a terrorist or corporate mogul or sports star, whatever suits your fancy. That person will be tortured and murdered for no other reason than because you wish it."

"This business we stop. Wherever this Dark Web place," Frankie said, "we close it down."

"It's not a real place like another bar," Bear said. "It's a bunch of sites on the internet with secret servers. Hard to find. Lily knows computers. She could probably tell us more. I'll ask her to research it." Bear heaved a huge sigh. "I gotta get to that bar to find out who drops the tapes off. Meanwhile, can your man keep tabs on this customer? See if he can find out exactly how the asshole places his orders?"

"Vinny?" Frankie asked.

"I assure you, ez already in the works."

Bear had no doubt the customer would soon be very sorry that he'd gone shopping. "And for God's sake, keep this from Lily or she'll want to go into that dive with me."

"Yes, *she* will."

Bear and Frankie looked around Vinny as he also turned. Behind him, Lily was parked in the doorway. Bear had no idea how much she'd overheard. "Crap. You're not going anywhere, Lily Gilbert."

"Oh, but I am." She jutted out her chin and narrowed her eyes.

Bear figured she'd spit fire if she could. "Don't go all dragon lady on me, Lily. You'd look a touch out of place in a cop bar, don't you think?"

"I'll drink rotgut wherever I want, thank you, Bear Jacobs. And now I'll go join Eunice for Scrabble." She maneuvered a wheelie and sped away.

"Double crap," Bear muttered, starting to rise.

"Let me go," Frankie said, leaning forward to pull himself up with his walker. "Maybe my little dove and I can reason with her about this dangerous idea."

Bear sat back down heavily and closed his eyes. He took a deep breath. This thing was getting uglier. He needed to call Clay, to ask if he'd take him to the bar.

"Of course he won't. I'm just a fuckin' old busybody," Bear muttered. But he'd call and leave a message about what had been discovered. He patted himself, looking for the pocket where he'd last put his phone. That's when he opened his eyes and saw Vinny still there, staring at him. Surprised, Bear said, "Ah ... I think Frankie's not coming back, Vinny."

"It is with you I wish an audience now, *Signore* Bear."

Now what?

"Sure. Shoot. I mean, what's on your mind?"

Vinny sat in the chair Frankie had vacated. "I understand that *Signora* Lily ez widow lady, and that you are her closest man friend."

What the hell?

"Yeah, I suppose you could say that. Far as I know."

"This makes you closest thing to a father of her daughter."

"Well, now just a minute ..."

"I know Sylvia spends much time with Tony Sapienza, and he ez maybe courting her."

"Ah, I don't think that is exactly the relationship ..."

"Nonetheless, she has expressed some interest in me. I am seeking your permission to court her myself."

"Hell, Vinny, you don't need my permission ..."

"But I cannot ask *Signora* Lily for this permission. She is a *woman*. This is a decision for the man of the family, I think."

"Vinny, you don't need anybody's permission to date Sylvia. I mean women these days ..."

"But Sylvia, she is a lady. She would expect a formal notification of interest, no?"

"Well, I ..."

"And Tony will be my rival for her favor. There is much competition for such a woman. It is only right."

"Speaking of Tony, you *do* know he's ..."

"Yes, he ez *padrone's* grandson. But *Signore* Sapienza understands these matters of the heart. Tony has not moved quickly enough, I think."

"No I guess he hasn't." Bear decided he was not going to be the one to tell Vinny the truth. As far as he was concerned, Tony's preferences were nobody's business but Tony's.

"So I may court Sylvia Henderson?"

"Yeah, sure. Go for it."

"You have filled my heart with joy, *Signore* Bear."

Yeah, and Lily's gonna fill my ears with words you've never heard from a lady before.

When Vinny left the room, Bear sat back to think. The Sapienza gang could shut down the ordering process, but it would take Bear to shut down the films. He knocked over the knight that he'd been about to capture. He drummed his fingers on the board. He started humming *Luck Be a Lady*. And he thought about his next move.

✦   ✦   ✦

When Vinny drove the residents home from the senior center later that afternoon, there was a noticeable silence in the front seat.

"We need to talk," Bear said to Lily.

"Not 'til we're home." She had no interest in sniping at him in front of the others. Her thoughts about that upcoming chit-chat flew out the window when the Caddy purred up the drive to Latin's Ranch. A small crowd was standing on the porch. They looked jolted wide-eyed, as if they'd taken hold of an electric fence together.

Rick Peters, their only male aide, had the stern facial planes of his Alaskan Alutiiq ancestors, but at the moment he looked startled. He was the tallest of the group, his height a gift from the Russian blood in his veins. Next to him in stature, Solana held a butcher knife. Next to her, Rosie wielded what looked for all the world like a long handled meat tenderizer. Behind the sisters, Ben's daughter, Rachael, was jiggling a howling BB up and down against her chest.

"Bear!" Lily yelped.

"What the hell is going on?" Bear snorted, coming instantly to attention from a light snooze. "Vinny, heads up."

As Bear struggled with the car door, Rick stepped forward on the porch to shout, "It's okay now. Everyone is okay."

"Ez trouble still here? Ez safe?" Vinny called to Rick then snapped at the residents, "Get back in car, everyone." Nobody listened to him, but Lily saw the gun appear from inside his coat.

Rick must have seen it, too. His ruddy complexion blanched as his voice changed to the soothing tone used with fractious patients. "It's safe now, Mr. Tononi. Ah, Vinny. Nobody's hurt. You can relax. No need for the gun. Really."

Lily had never seen such alarm on Rick's face. The girls looked ashen, too. Apparently a goomba with a hand cannon was scarier than whatever had spooked them to begin with.

"Rick," Bear commanded. "Tell me."

Everyone stood or leaned on their canes or sat in their wheelchairs while Rick told his story. Lily watched Vinny get even stonier and Bear squint until his beady eyes almost disappeared behind his cheeks. Charlie squirmed in his chair, no doubt seeking a comfy position for his privates. Frankie consoled a fluttery Eunice. Lily sensed her own face was the portrait of alarm.

"I was in the kitchen, tenderizing the meat for Aurora's Swiss steak," Rick began. "That's a whole lot of pounding for her to do on her own, to feed all of us. So I offered to help. While I worked, I saw Solana and Rosie through the kitchen window, picking blackberries on the edge of the pasture."

It was warm in the sun. Lily noticed the girls had removed their hoodies. Their young bodies looked fit and strong in their t-shirts. Rick would have glanced through the window plenty often. From his point of view, the scenery must have been quite stunning.

"Something caught the corner of my eye. A movement. I turned to the woods and saw a stranger staring at the girls. I grabbed up a butcher knife and beat it out the back door screaming, 'Hey! Hey you!'"

"That's right," Solana nodded, her voice high with excitement. "That's what we heard. Well, except Rick yelled 'Hey! Hey you, *shithead.*'"

Rosie chimed in. "Solana and I didn't see anybody except Rick running toward the woods with kitchen utensils. We thought that was kinda strange, but then we think a lot of stuff around here is kinda strange."

Rick continued. "The guy looked at me charging toward him and disappeared back into the forest. By the time I got to the tree line, he was gone from sight. I didn't know where to go so I stopped. That's when I realized I still had the meat tenderizer as well as the knife.

"Solana and Rosie ran up to me, asked what I was yelling about. I told them I'd seen some jerk sneaking around in the woods. I gave them each one of the weapons for protection, you know? Then we all stared toward the woods, looking for any sign of the guy."

Solana said, "We were pretty scared -"

"I wasn't," Rick muttered.

"- but we really jumped when Folly flew past us into the forest, yapping for all his worth. Rick yelled for him to come back, but the dog didn't stop."

Rosie said, "Then we heard a car engine start and the squeal of tires. Solana said it sounded like the guy was leaving. Whoever it was."

"Folly finally came back, thank God," Rick said. "I'd rather take on that stranger empty-handed than lose Jessica's dog."

"We thought maybe it was just a homeless guy looking for a place to hole up. Then we realized that wasn't likely," Solana added. "He had a car waiting out on the road. Or somebody with him did.'

"We walked back to the house. I let Aurora and Rachael know what happened and that everything was okay. Then we heard a car turn in the drive. I thought it was the mystery car coming. The girls kept their weapons in case, and we went out to the porch." Rick paused to smile. "I'm damn glad it was you guys coming home. And that's the whole story. Just some losers casing us, I suppose. Maybe thinking about breaking in. They won't be back. My little gang here showed them the exit, right ladies?"

Rosie and Solana smiled, but Ben's daughter Rachael rolled her eyes, said, "Whatever," and walked over to the seniors.

"Bear can you do something with BB? He likes you better than me." She unloaded the squalling baby then walked back into the house.

"Can you describe the man?" Bear asked Rick, tucking BB into the crook of one arm so he could balance his weight on his quad cane.

"Not much ... all I remember is that he had long arms, was big in the chest. Like maybe a wrestler. And he had red hair. Copper-colored."

Solana looked at Lily who looked at Bear. A barrel-chested guy with red hair. Lily guessed they all three knew it was the Ape.

Solana asked, "How did they know where we are?"

"I thought I felt eyes on us out there in the woods at the homeless camp," Lily answered.

"They must have had a car in the lot at the county park," Bear said, jiggling the baby who was now merrily hiccupping. "Followed us home. Waited for most of us to be gone before creeping up."

Solana and her sister had been found.

CHAPTER EIGHT

Case Notes
September 19, 7 p.m.

I'm glad Jessica and Ben are camping out in the mountains tonight and know nothing about the Ape spying on the girls. We don't have to answer questions about the mob of mobsters now surrounding Sam's old trailer. Frankie had them here in the time it would take to bake a cannoli. He told us they'd stay until the sisters left. Then he added that, even afterwards, some would be around but invisible to the naked eye. I take it he meant they'd be on watch from the woods. A hostile famiglia *doesn't necessarily know Frankie is here, not from events so far. But they must be getting close.*

We all sat with the sisters in the Latin's Ranch living room until the Sapienza army arrived. No doubt about it, Solana was scared by what had happened. Her instinct was to take Rosie and run. Bear comforted them by pointing out they weren't that important any more (I've mentioned before what a sweet talker he can be). He said now that they've been found among people, not just hiding by themselves in the woods, the bad guys know Solana has already told all she knows. She isn't a threat anymore. Unless the Ape has a personal vendetta against her, the girls are likely out of danger.

Just to be sure, Frankie promised them new digs by tomorrow night. In another place, pretty much of their choice. He'll arrange for their departure this afternoon; they'll probably be gone by the time Jessica gets home.

*After Frankie's thugs took up their posts around the Airstream for
the night, the two girls retired. Everyone in the house went to bed early, too, tuckered out from all the excitement. Everyone except Bear
and me. We hung back a bit. We had things to say to each other.*

Lily Gilbert, Safety Monitor for PI Bear Jacobs

It was late. Bear and Lily stopped outside the door to Bear and Charlie's room. Bear's chestnut quad cane *kachunked* to a halt. He'd had the
heavy-duty device custom made to support his size. It even held a very
sharp surprise within the beautiful wooden shaft. Lily always figured the
hidden dagger had been more or less a doff of the hat to Bear's sense of
humor, at least until it had saved his life one scary night not long ago.

Lily's wheelchair moved quietly except when she whizzed along at
great speed. But noise wasn't really an issue, since Charlie could sleep
through a pep rally. There was no need to whisper.

Leaning on his cane with one massive hand and putting the other on
the door knob, Bear said, "Lily, I ¬– "

"Shut it," she snapped.

He did.

She continued, pointing a finger in his direction. "You're gonna tell me
you need to go to that cop bar and pretend that you are a has-been PI re-
visiting a scene from your youth where you'll try to purchase a snuff film,
and that my being there would only put you in danger by calling too much
attention to you, and that I'd make anybody suspicious what with being a
frail old woman and all. And, Bear, of course it makes more sense for you
to go with Clay than with me. You don't have to say anymore about it because I'm not operating with a noggin full of gumballs. I know that you're
right so there's nothing to fight about. I just want to be asked, I want to be
considered, but I don't want to be so obstinate as to be an old fool. Got it?"

He never cracked a smile, just nodded. "Okay. But I was actually going
to ask you about your leg. I want to know what the doctor had to say."

"Oh that!" Lily smiled broadly. She told him about her trip to the clinic, the good news about a prosthesis, and finally, she admitted to her fear of failure. These old friends knew a lot about making a body do what it no longer thought it could. Both had faced down physical demons in order to maneuver at all.

"You'll do what's best. Don't want to get all mushy or make your head swell or anything, but you're a sensible girl."

Lily felt her cheeks warm with the sort-of compliment. "Speaking of sensible. I think I need to help the sisters tomorrow. Frankie will take care of them okay, I know that. But they'll be happier with a woman around, at least until they're on their way to wherever they're going."

"Good plan."

"Then I'm going to bed." She reached way up to pat his grizzled cheek. "You be on your guard tomorrow."

"Yes, ma'am. But, ah, Lily? There's just one more thing."

"Can it wait, Bear? I'm tired."

"Vinny asked me for permission to court Sylvia, and I gave it to him. Good night!" He escaped into his room before Lily could quit sputtering.

Faced with the closed door, Lily turned her chair and wheeled toward her own room. She'd get the whole story out of Bear sooner or later. In fact, she already knew that Sylvia had heard from Vinny earlier in the evening. Her middle-aged daughter had sounded like a lovesick teen when she called.

Lily rang for Alita, the aide on duty, to help her prepare for the night. Then she began the slow, arduous process of transferring across a board from her wheelchair to the hospital bed. A prosthetic leg would make this chore obsolete. Wouldn't that be something?

While she struggled with the nightly task, she thought back to her husband, Harmon. He'd died not two months after his daughter's birth. Syl's first name was Harmony, in his honor. With a fatherless baby and an itch to start life over and over again, Lily had moved from place to place, sampling like a honey bee. Maybe that was why Sylvia had fought so hard against change all of her life. One career, one house, one boyfriend who later became her one husband. Syl stuck with Kyle through thick and some pretty skeletal thin, if one partner being gay could be said to stretch the bonds of a marriage. All in all, Lily had been glad to hear how happy Sylvia sounded on the phone.

But Vinny? Mr. Concealed Weaponry? Oh well, at least he was loyal to the people he liked. He'd broken a few laws on behalf of their sorry old asses. If Sylvia wanted to be one of the people he liked, Lily needed to butt out. Not her strong suit, but she had to try.

By the time Alita arrived to help her remove her day clothes and don a nightgown, Lily had made it onto the side of the bed and was sitting there waiting.

Another battle won.

✦ ✦ ✦

As Bear prepared for his outing, he was relieved he didn't have to worry about Lily. She understood that a young lawman like Clay Galligan would make a better partner in a cop bar than she would. Clay had Irish blood in his veins so he'd be right at home at The Abbey. What Bear didn't tell Lily was that he hadn't yet connected with the deputy. Instead, the two men had played a perfectly executed game of phone tag. As much as Bear hated the cell phone, he'd managed to leave a message. Clay had called back when the big man was in the shower that morning. Of course, when Bear called again Clay was out, so he left the deputy a message to meet him at the bar if he could.

Bear was well aware he wasn't a top priority for the deputy. Clay thought of him as a pest, meddling in official affairs. And Bear had to face it. He'd have felt the same way about a relic shamus when he was Clay's age.

Now Bear had a choice. He could go to The Abbey alone, try to strike up a conversation to pass around the story that he was a has-been PI with an axe to grind against shyster lawyers. Any fucker in a three piece suit and alligator shoes. Boy, would he like to see someone like that brought down to size.

Whaddaya call a dead lawyer? A good start.

Sure he could go alone, but it didn't feel smart. He needed a sidekick for cover. Someone to listen to his loud ranting, help stir up conversation with others in the bar. It would be gravy if that sidekick also doubled Bear's odds of survival.

That was the biggest problem created by Clay's absence. Bear didn't want to involve anyone else in something so potentially dangerous. Not Sam. Not Rick. Not Charlie. So he would have to go alone. His whole plan depended on a cop drinking in The Abbey who might recognize him from his private investigator days. That was his best credential. Cops would accept him and believe he was as disgusted with lawyers as they usually were.

Bear sure as hell no longer looked like the young PI who had the respect of law enforcement even when he was working to prove them wrong. He wasn't called Bear back then. He was heavier now, slower and, face it, crippled. A brown fringe of hair shot through with silver gray hid the jowly face that had always been more appealing than handsome. Only his dark, penetrating eyes looked the same as they had in his youth.

Bear thought about ways he could be recognized. Well, he'd always hummed old standards when he was working out a plan. Still did. That was a 'tell' he could use if anyone in the bar remembered him.

And one more thing. He ambled to his closet and yanked a heavy winter robe off the top shelf to get to the boot box stored up there behind it. Hooking his fingers under the lid, he pulled the box down, catching it against his chest. Bear placed it on his bed and began spreading out the contents. A bundle of letters. He could still smell a hint of their perfume over the cherry smokiness of three beautiful old pipes. An ancient wallet, pocket knife, binoculars, a manila envelope stuffed with papers. When he picked a photo album out of the box, several black and whites fell along with the corner mounts that had long since lost their glue. Memories fluttered across his bedspread. Bear returned the scallop-edged snapshots to the box, trying not to look at them.

Under a number of old notebooks – the kind reporters or stenos used to use – he found what he'd been looking for. In the noir movies, dicks had worn fedoras. But this was Washington. So Bear had always donned a floppy rain hat while working outdoors. It was frayed and smelled of stale sweat. On its brim was an embroidered letter R knocking a ball out of the park. It was the logo of the old Seattle Rainiers, Bear's team long before the Mariners came to be. Maybe, just maybe somebody would see it, recognize it.

With fondness, he slapped the hat against his leg to reshape it and knock off any dust. He put it on the bed while he reloaded the boot box, shoved it back on the closet shelf and replaced the wool robe that hid it. He patted his pockets. Phone, ID, billfold. Check. The afternoon was cool, and he may not return until late so he put on his navy windbreaker. Finally, Bear placed the ridiculous old hat on his head, went out the back way, mounted Sitting Bull, and headed for the road that would take him to town and The Abbey.

Before he was half way up the drive, he could see his plan was thwarted. A rumbling Chevy truck, parked directly across the entrance to Latin's Ranch, blocked his exit. A golf cart could get around it, Bear supposed, but not if the truck driver rolled forward or back. The Bull would get crushed.

"Damn it all to hell," Bear roared to the trees and bushes along the drive. "That woman." He came to a stop at the truck.

The truck driver shut down the Silverado's motor, jumped down from the cab, and sauntered toward the golf cart, his hands shoved into the pockets of his jeans and his cowboy hat hiding his eyes.

"Lily put you up to this, didn't she?" Bear barked.

"I ain't no squealer," Sam answered.

"I don't want you to be part of it," Bear said. "I'm not kidding around, Sam. Move the truck."

"I ain't the kind to leave a friend in need, neither."

"Move the fuckin' truck."

"Well, now. Let's consider what you can do about it. Maybe you could whine to Jessica that I'm abusive when she's gone. That might get me fired. But no, she'd rather see you abused than keep me away from her horses."

Bear changed tactics. "You could find yourself alone on poker night."

"Hell, Bear, where else you gonna drink beer and smoke cigars?"

"I'm doing this alone, Sam."

"I reckon you just have to take me with you, or you don't go at all."

Crap.

Bear had no choice but to acquiesce. Besides, like it or not, Bear needed the help. But that *need*, that emasculation. He'd always worked alone. Admitting he wasn't the man he used to be was never easy. The older he got, the more often it happened.

Maybe Sam read his mind. Or maybe Sam, with no place to go but an old Airstream on somebody else's ranch, maybe he knew a thing or two about loss. Either way, Sam said, "Together we're a formidable enough team to make punks think a time or two. That includes punk cops."

Without another word, Bear returned Sitting Bull to the house and plugged it into its charging station. Sam followed behind him so all Bear had to do when he was done with the cart was clamber up into the Silverado.

Sam said, "This whole thing disgusts me as much as it does you. Thanks for not cutting me out."

"Yeah, sure."

"And Bear?"

"At the bar, call me Al. Or Jacobs."

"Sure. But Bear? Is that the prototype for the ass hat I hear tell about?"

That was it for conversation for most of the drive as they headed toward The Abbey. Finally, Sam asked, "So a guy picked up a snuff DVD at this bar. Now you're hoping to find who drops them off."

"Yep. 'Cause that guy can tell us who's making them."

"You just order up your favorite type of victim, right?" Sam mimicked a phone call. "'Lo? My boss just fired me. Do you have something in a white middle-aged executive, size 44 tall, available for jamming head first into a giant shredder?"

Bear joined the macabre game. "I want a punk like the shit who stole my car. Plus a teenage tease, you know, one of those slutty diva singers."

Sam wrinkled his brow as he turned his truck into The Abbey's parking area. He maneuvered around pot holes filled with mud. Rain had been alternating with sun most of the day. Washingtonians called it sun showers. As he parked, with the truck nose pointing outward, Sam said, "One thing I don't get, Bear. Say you want someone to die. Why not just do it yourself? Or order a hit from a guy like Vinny?"

"Just a guess, Sam. No matter how angry we get, most of us won't pull a trigger ourselves."

"Always preferred taking care of my own troubles," Sam muttered.

"And I imagine these films cost some less than a hit. They probably make a bunch of them at a time. Keep duplicates to sell again and again as the same victim types are requested. Need more answers to know for sure." Bear slid out of the truck.

One thing he *did* know for sure. He was very happy to have Sam at his side.

✦   ✦   ✦

Bear burst through the door of The Abbey, leaning on Sam the way one drunk supports another, loudly humming *Whiskey in the Jar*. He felt the old folk song would be appropriate for an Irish pub. When two other patrons shouted in unison, "Shut the fuck up," he was thrilled to have the opening he needed.

"I'm older than all you rookie pant pissers put together so pipe down," he shouted back as Sam steered him toward the bar. "I was a shamus back when you were still at your mama's titties." Bear hoisted one old cheek onto a bar stool, then the other. He set his quad cane against the brass foot rail. Sam stood right beside him.

It was early enough in the day that the bar wasn't packed. But lawmen, whether county, state or fed, work odd hours. A cop bar was never empty. The bartender put down the mug he was drying, slapped the towel onto the bar top and walked down to Sam. "Your friend's already had a bit too much, don't you think?"

"Hell, no. He's an ornery old bastard, mad at the world just now. Hardly started on booze at all. Whadddaya say, Al? Pints all around?"

"Abso-fuckin-lutely," Bear said. He peered around the bar. It was dark, with neon beer signs blocking what little natural light might come in the windows. Old wooden booths, tables with mismatched chairs, a beautifully carved bar. Above the backlit booze bottles was a wide screen TV showing a soccer game with no sound. At one end of the bar, another monitor cycled through photos of the bar food, events The Abbey sponsored, and customers in various stages of drunkenness. Bear looked back to the bartender. "Thought Les Carnahan ran this joint. 'Course, I been gone a while."

"He still does. That's me. The one you remember is my dad. He started the business." Carnahan was tall, shoulders slouched in the way of many aging athletes. As he pulled the tap handle, filling one mug after another, he said, "And who might you be?"

"Name's Jacobs. Al Jacobs. People call me Bear these days."

Carnahan glanced at him and chuckled. "Guess I can see why." His smile creased his cheeks into laugh lines but humor did not reach his eyes.

Bear watched him and wondered. Did the bartender know what was in the packages? Money, drugs, movies? Probably not. Bars got used for drops, but questions rarely got asked. It was the way things worked. He said, "Used to be a PI back in the day. Worked with the sheriffs and the city cops back then. They drank here. I drank here."

"They still do. So welcome back, Al Jacobs." Carnahan set mugs in front of Bear and Sam.

"I'll be goddamned," said a shaky voice from one of the tables. "I remember that name. And that crappy Rainiers hat. Always wondered if you was bald as an eagle under it. Never seen you without it."

Bear stared at the speaker. The hair on his neck warned him this guy was bad news. He rumbled. "I know you, too, you old bastard. Seattle cop. Connors, ain't it?" He left the barstool and carried his mug over to the table, Sam following along. "Join you?"

"Free country. Used to be anyway."

Bear cocked his head. "Don't get your meaning."

"Til the spics and ragheads took over everything."

Bear recalled now why Connors affected him like a bad odor. As they took chairs, Bear began to introduce Sam. He had a moment of panic realizing he hadn't made up an alias, and nobody here should know Sam's real name. "This here is … ah … Horse Smith."

"Strange handle."

"Ah, yeah," Sam agreed, eyeing Bear. "It is at that." He dipped his chin in the direction of Connors, the brim of his cowboy hat obscuring his eyes.

The three talked trash about the old days, when Connors worked a case while Bear, then a defensive lawyer's investigator, worked against him. They swore and chortled and as the afternoon grew long, others joined. A waitress came on duty, and started doling out bowls of chips and rounds of ale. According to her name tag, she was Ginger. Bear, never one to miss a lady's assets, noticed that the tag on her ample chest also read, in much smaller type, "Not that it's any business of yours."

She was a leggy redhead, now thick in the body. Ginger had seen more than a few years of passing out pitchers. Her arm muscles looked solid as those of a riveter on a WWII war poster. Her wild red curls were pulled back in a rubber band, gray showing in the roots. The wrinkles that touched her eyes and her lips were spattered with freckles. Ginger alone might have noticed how Bear and Sam slowed down their intake as the others increased. While the drinking fest went on, she cast more than one glance Bear's way, even raising an eyebrow at him.

Bear finally felt the audience was in the right frame of mind. He slammed down a mug, silencing the rest. "You want my opinion, it's lawyers who fucked up the law. A dick, private or not, can't do nothin' anymore without some mouthpiece screamin' foul. It was a piece of shit like that who ended my career. Had my license pulled 'cause I went a little far with an interrogation, if you know what I mean."

The others generally agreed.

Horse Smith said, "Bet you'd like to see a bastard like that strung up by his balls."

Al Jacobs answered, "Yeah, I'd pay a lot to see something like that."

The others agreed again.

Bear stood, wobbled and leaned on his sidekick. "Gotta get back home," he slobbered. Then he belched.

"You mean back to *the* home?" Connors jeered. More laughter and old age wisecracks. By the time Bear struggled back into Sam's Silverado, he was disgusted by the whole scene. Well, maybe not by Ginger.

"I tell you, Sam. Whenever I get down in the dumps, remind me of this. Latin's Ranch is a paradise compared to hanging with a bunch of drunks, recalling their glory days."

"We coming back tomorrow?"

"Yeah. We've set the bait. Gotta see who bites. May take a day. May take a week. After that, I'd say it's a waste of time. Maybe Keegan will pick up a lead out there at the camp. Or we try something else."

✦ ✦ ✦

Lily and Eunice rode to SeaTac in the limo along with the two sisters. Solana and Rosie had stuffed their things into their backpacks. They looked edgy but eager to be on their way. This area of the country had not been kind to them; they needed a new start a long way from the Ape and the homeless camp. Frankie willingly provided it for them.

Lily smiled at the colorful scarf each wore, Solana's in her hair and Rosie's around the waist of her jeans like a sash. The bright silk patterns came from the large stock in Eunice's wardrobe. Lily wouldn't be surprised if they each also had a hand crocheted, sequin spattered pouch with several bills. Eunice was like that.

The only visible thing the girls hand carried was a waxed bag of the chipotle cornmeal-encrusted fried chicken that Aurora had made for them to eat on the plane. Lily smelled the luscious aroma. She imagined the rest of the airline passengers would swoon from hunger. Or offer up more bills for one taste.

At the moment, Eunice was going through a list of warnings for the girls. "... call if you need anything at all ... keep cash in your shoe ... if a stranger gets too friendly, slap him silly ..." Lily stopped listening. She knew that Solana was twice as street smart as Eunice had ever been. Solana would never call, never need to be told how to hide cash, never again allow a stranger within her territorial imperative if she could help it. Eunice appeared to believe this was a temporary good-bye, that the girls would return to her loving circle one day. They were merely off on an adventure.

Lily knew it was forever. Nobody could know where Solana and Rosie were headed except Frankie and the girls themselves. Well, maybe Vinny, too, but it would be easier to dig the secret out of the La Brea tar pits. Lily took Eunice's papery thin hand and held it tightly.

At the airport, the youngsters hugged the two women. "You're like having grammas," Solana said. "We'll never forget you." Vinny escorted the girls to the check-in counter of Delta, then bowed slightly, turned and walked back toward the Caddy. Sitting safely inside it, the old friends could see the girls through the enormous airport windows. They watched as Solana and Rosie disappeared from sight, down the corridor past the escalators. Life would not be smooth sailing for them, but Frankie's good graces gave them a fighting chance.

Eunice broke cover. "Thank you, Lily, for not telling me I shouldn't get my hopes up. How can a little hope ever hurt?" She squeezed Lily's hand. "I know they'll never be back. And we'll never know where they've gone."

For all that Eunice projected jingling, colorful, perfumed bubble-head-edness, Lily knew the depth of her friend. Eunice faced down pain and sorrow on a daily basis but rarely let on to the others how hard she knew life could be. Lily shook her head. "No, my dear. We won't. Not good for them. Not good for us."

Eunice added, "I just hate stories with no endings."

They settled into silence, watching the Seattle scenery as the limo crawled up I-5 in yet another traffic fiasco. Lily thought that if Eunice hadn't come along for the ride, she could have used this time to quiz Vinny about his interest in Sylvia. Maybe that was another story whose ending was not hers to see.

Back at Latin's Ranch, Eunice went to their room and Lily wheeled her-self toward Jessica's office. The caregiver would be back from her trail ride by now. Lily had promised that she would tell Jessica the next time she was getting into a sticky situation. Jessica had promised to let her make her own decisions but had sworn she might come along if Lily's path looked dangerous. It was high time to bring Jess up to speed on Bear's pub crawl, and Jo Keegan out there in the woods. Keegan and Jessica, similar in age, in independence, and in their penchants to protect others, were becoming friends. It would be a flip of a coin between Jessica and Lily who would out-worry whom over the cop's wellbeing.

CHAPTER NINE

Case Notes
September 20, 3 p.m.

*When Jessica Winslow was my home caregiver, she never made me
feel that my mind was giving up along with my body. We grew close
and stayed that way when I went to a nursing home. Jess and Sylvia
hatched the plan to start an adult care facility, and here we all are at
Latin's Ranch. Well, okay, maybe I had something to do with hatching that plan, too.*

*I love Jess. She kept me alive, saw Sylvia through the loss of Kyle,
and we've both returned the favor, helping Jessica flourish in the af-
termath of her own loss. I'd say the three of us are a sort of extended family, a mother/daughter with an adopted daughter/little sister.
Something like that.*

*Anyhoo, we went from her office out to the patio which was sort of
a Grand Central on this jewel of a day. Jessica and I sat in the deck
chairs. She'd brought along a stack of new DVDs and began removing the outer plastic and multiple stickers. Arthritic hands can't get
into the damn things at all so we'd never see movies if somebody
didn't crack them open for us.*

*It was almost shawl weather. The morning showers had stopped mo-
mentarily, giving way to autumn sun. I took a deep breath of the
clean air which would become too brisk as the afternoon progressed.
Mornings and evenings in Western Washington are almost always*

cool, no matter how warm the day.

Pots of colorful mums dot our patio. I tend to them, but container gardening is all I can manage these days; I've mentioned before that Jessica doesn't like it when I call it pot gardening. I admit I'd like to try some of that 'pot for medicinal reasons.' Hell, here in Washington it's legal if I just want to return to my hippy dippy days.

Charlie was washing the bird cage. He takes care of the canaries so that our aides don't have to bother with it. We all try to pitch in now and then, to do our bit. Feeling useful is a main ingredient in feeling good. While Charlie scrubs what he calls their manor house, he leaves the birdies indoors in a smaller cage. He refers to that as their getaway cabin.

Aurora was building a fire in the grill at the other end of the patio. She refuses to use lighter fluid saying it adds a bad taste, but it makes starting the fire something of an extreme sport. At the moment, she was muttering at the charcoal in what I assume was an ancient Spanish curse.

"Something smoky for dinner tonight," Jessica said. She was peeling off a strip of clear plastic that was clinging to her palm.

"Carne asada with a corn casserole," I answered. I always look at the daily menu first thing in the morning. All of us do. Charlie once said dinner is the main thing he still looks forward to now that the Missus is gone. Some of us think he's better off without her, but that's another story.

Jessica looked up from her task. "Okay, Lily. What have you been up to?"

I began. She listened to me carefully, like she always does. She already knew about Solana and Rosie, of course, and she'd heard about Rick's encounter with the stranger in the woods. I filled her in on the snuff films, Bear's vigil at the bar, Clay's request to Sheriff Delacruz about an undercover operation, Keegan's placement at the homeless camp. I wanted to minimize Frankie's participation. But if Jess didn't already know she was housing a capo, it was time she did. So I told her that, too.

When I finished, we sat for a longish while. She sighed, looking off into the distance. *"Wonder if gangsters are watching from the woods right now."* Nothing like that was visible. Folly was trying to sleep in sunny spots, but Furball kept forcing him from one to another. A V of squabbling geese momentarily interrupted the silence as they practiced for their flight south. At the barn, Ben led Gina Lola out into the pasture to take a walk. The old horse had belonged to his grandfather, and while she pulled loads no more, she still enjoyed a stroll along the fence line where the other horses might have missed juicy tidbits.

Jessica spoke to the distance. *"It would be nice if it were always peaceful like this. I'd rather you'd all just stay put. But life doesn't work that way."* She looked at me with a weary smile. *"You're not prisoners. But you're my responsibility, nonetheless. If it looks like any of you are in danger, come to me. I'll help set things straight however I can."*

Now I ask you. Who wouldn't love a person like that? It really is too bad I scare the snot out of her so much of the time.

- Lily Gilbert, Grateful Assistant to PI Bear Jacobs

Deputy Jo Keegan was warm in the sunny meadow. She fought back a yawn and lectured herself to stay on the alert as she wiped sweat from under her bangs, leaving a trail of dust across her forehead. She pulled off the faded purple UDub hoodie, threw it aside and continued marking off her next cut.

It was her third day at the homeless camp. She'd thought she'd be bored by now, so far from her office and case load. Instead, she was enjoying a stint of physical labor although her shoulders ached from the work. Years ago, her dad had taught her enough general carpentry to be a fair-to-middling framer. Now she recalled those lessons. From the odds and ends of lumber that the camp had accumulated, she had repaired the old picnic table and the pallets that supported the tents. At the moment she was building a couple of benches. A few of the kids liked to help out. She'd tried to put one of them on spider patrol, but she'd received a lecture on how good the eight-legged monsters were for the environment.

The Tent Master, Rita, had given her the tent that had been home to Solana and Rosie before they evacuated the camp. After that, Keegan and Rita stayed apart, not wanting anyone to catch wind of their association. Keegan's eagerness to help with chores quickly got her close to the others in the camp, and her affable nature lured them into feeling at ease. Shy and mistrustful at first, they began to smile, stop for a chat, offer her wild blackberries. They seemed to buy her cover story, that she was recently unemployed, down on her luck, but sure to bounce back before long.

Keegan observed them closely and asked about disappearances, but none of the camp members seemed upset or on guard about her questions. If anything, they were resigned to disappearance as a fact of life in this segment of society. None of them fit the description of Joey the Ape nor looked like any kind of gangland muscle.

Keegan stretched her back then picked up the hammer and drove a ten-penny nail into the seat of the bench. Maybe she'd use the cell phone to call Clay tonight. She'd have to go alone, into the woods far enough for nobody to overhear. First, though, she'd get her gun from Rita's tent. They'd hidden it there in case anyone tossed the newbie's quarters. That kind of thing was common in a camp like this.

Keegan wanted to know what Clay might have discovered about the films, and whether Bear and Lily were frustrating him. The thought of his impatience with them made her grin. He was so ill-equipped to deal with citizenry that flouted his authority. Not that she'd ever say it out loud, but she agreed with Lily that he was a bit tight assed.

Then another thought hit her as the sun and labor continued to make her sweat. Maybe she'd even go as far as the county park to make her call. Then she could also wash with hot water. It was the noise she was making with the hammer, and maybe her wandering thoughts, that masked other sound. The voice was very close behind her when it said, "Freeze, bitch."

The cold metal at the back of her head could only be a gun barrel. She did as she was told, but every muscle and all her training rushed to full alert.

Her hand tensed on the hammer.

"Drop it now," the voice commanded. The barrel shoved harder against her skull.

Again, she did as she was told, tossing the hammer to the ground.

"Flat down. On your fuckin' face." A hand pushed roughly down on her shoulder.

She followed the order, tucking her hands underneath her belly. The warmth from her work morphed to an icicle chill. The hammer was picked up by a second person who threw it into the wood pile.

At least they aren't gonna crack my skull with it.

"Arms out to the sides."

She was grabbed roughly, her wrists positioned one on the other, and a plastic zip tie was applied tightly enough to bind. Then two of them picked her up by her elbows.

The voice growled in her ear. She felt body heat and smelled fetid breath. "A lady cop. A real one. Somebody's gonna pay through the nose to see you cut down to size."

She threw back her head, trying to connect with the man behind her, but he dodged her effort. In the process, she turned just enough to see two of the camp children watching from a distance, their eyes and mouths wide open. But children like these had seen violence before. Neither screamed. "Go tell Rita," she yelled to them. A hand clouted her so hard her ear rang.

She was hauled, kicking wildly at her captors, into the woods. One of them would be limping for some time to come. Blackberry whips grabbed at her ankles and cut the skin on her arms.

"Careful, asshole," one captor sniped at the other. "Don't mark her."

Flooded with adrenalin and fear, Keegan had one question that terrified her more than all the others.

How do they know I'm a cop?

✦　✦　✦

If their second visit to The Abbey had any result, Bear and Sam didn't detect it. Nobody appeared to recognize the retired PI so starting a conversation was not as easy as the first day. Bear loudly told Sam he'd like to see someone take down a scumbag shyster, but nobody paid any attention, other than the bartender and the waitress. Bear saw them exchange a glance and shrug at each other.

Finally, Ginger yelled to the room at large, "Any you doughnut commandos know this gumshoe? He's lookin' for old pals."

"Who you callin' a doughnut commando, girlie?" one scruffy drinker yelled back.

"If the shoe fits," Ginger retorted, patting the heckler's rotund belly with one hand as she hip-switched by, five beer mugs clutched by their handles in the other.

On day three, Bear changed his humming to *The Wild Rover* if for no other reason than he was sick of *Whiskey in the Jar*.

"Thank God," Ginger said landing pints in front of Bear and Sam. "Thought I was gonna scream if you didn't change your tune."

Bear laughed.

Ginger looked around the room. As Bear watched, she made some sort of decision. She lowered her voice saying, "I don't know why you're here. Neither does Les." She cocked her head in the direction of the bartender whose back was turned while he stocked a cooler. "But I figure you ain't found what you're looking for or you wouldn't still be here."

Horse Smith tipped the brim of his hat. "Seems to me you're a mighty thoughty filly."

"Can the crap, cowboy," she shot back at him. ""Why are you two here?"

Now Bear had a decision to make. She could blow the whole thing. Or she could help. "We're looking for a guy who drops off a certain kind of package. Size of a DVD. Not interested in any other kind of, ah, delivery that might be going on around here."

Ginger stared icy bullets at him. "You haven't learned by your age what's none of your business?"

"I've learned what's slime. I've learned you can't always kick evil under a rug and pretend you don't see it."

Ginger's eyes got a little greener. A blush worked its way into her cheeks. "You got balls, I'll give you that." She turned and went back to work. At one point, as she went to the end of the bar to place orders, Bear saw her whisper to the bartender who'd inherited the joint from his father ... and apparently its drop box status. A bar had little recourse once the mob decided it was a stop for protection money, bets, you name it. Carnahan glanced at Bear, then turned his back once more.

The next time Ginger came to their table she said, "Move over to the bar. Watch the monitor with our menu and pictures of our customers. Your boy is on it. If you happen to recognize him, nothing Les and I can do about it, right? Nobody could hold us responsible." She walked away.

"Bear?" Sam asked.

"Wait until we finish these mugs. Don't want our move to the bar connected to her." Sam nodded and began a long story that would bore a shaggy dog. Finally, Bear struggled up, waited for his balance to settle on the quad cane, and the two moved to bar stools. They ordered shots, which neither drank. But it was the price to watch the video at the bar without drawing attention to themselves.

Images dissolved one to another. Shots of burgers, meat pies, fried cheese, and other pub foods. Interspersed were pictures of The Abbey Little League team, St. Patty's day shenanigans, and regular customers laughing or mugging at the camera.

Time passed.

"Boring. Just as soon watch soccer with no sound," Sam cocked his head toward the game on the television but kept his eyes on the rotating pictures.

Then Bear froze. Sam did, too. The photo on the monitor was a guy big in the chest, long armed, with hair so coppery red he looked like an orangutan. But it wasn't the Ape that made Bear's blood ice in his veins. It was the Ape's arm around a cop. A deputy sheriff.

Ape was laughing with Clay Galligan.

Sam grabbed Bear's shoulder as the tape rotated on. "Wasn't that ..."

The big man looked back at Sam, suddenly incapable of a deep breath. "It ..." His phone interrupted him. Bear found it in his left pants pocket. He'd put Keegan's prepaid phone in his contact list. The call came from "Cupcake." Answering the insistent beep, he shouted an urgent command. "Get out, Keegan. Get out of there now."

The caller wasn't Keegan. It was Rita. "Bear, they got her. Deputy Keegan is gone."

Instantly, all faded. Bear felt he was looking through the wrong end of the telescope. His head pounded with the bar noise, now overwhelming.

But in a flash, he rallied. He had to act. Everything needed doing at once. Everything. "First, we get out of this fucking bar," Bear said heading for the door, no longer with any pretense of drunkenness. Sam threw a fifty onto the counter then raced out to the truck, arriving at the same time as the big man.

"We going to the camp?" Sam asked. He gestured backwards with a thumb. "I have Winnie in the tool box."

"No. I'm too old, too slow. Head home." Bear rang Lily. His enormous fingers made the task slow, infuriating. While Bear waged war with the phone, Sam gunned the Silverado out of the parking lot bounding through potholes and mud onto the street. The sky looked like it was about to open with a serious afternoon squall.

When Lily answered, Bear blurted, "Clay is the link, Lily. Clay Galligan. I never saw it." He told her what had happened at the bar.

"But … but … why? I mean maybe money I guess, but endanger Keegan? She's his partner!"

"No time to think on it just now, Lily. Get to Sheriff Delacruz. I'm betting Clay never told him about the undercover operation. And we've only worked through Clay. Delacruz doesn't know where Keegan went. Only we do. Keep calling. Don't tell anyone else … another cop could be a rogue."

"Got it," she promised.

"In the meantime, Lily, be careful."

"Why?"

"Because we know what Clay is up to. And the fucker can't stand for that."

"We're in danger?"

"I'm calling Frankie next to increase vigilance at the Ranch. And to find Keegan."

As Bear called Frankie, he worried he should have made this call first. Bad guys always mobilize faster than good cops. Frankie told him Vinny would connect with Ghost by the time Bear and Sam got back. And he'd add a couple guards to Latin's Ranch.

The Silverado raced past stores, homes, then fields like a thoroughbred thundering down the home stretch. Somewhere along the line, rain burst loose with force, the way it does in the Pacific Northwest.

Bear's suffering was a physical ache, like a fist to the gut. He couldn't breathe right. Keegan was in trouble. And he'd put her there.

Sam braked hard. The big truck screeched around the corner and into the Latin's Ranch drive on two wheels. He apologized as it righted itself. "I'll try not to kill us before we get there."

"Anything happens to Keegan, I'll wish you had."

CHAPTER TEN

Case Notes
September 20, 8 p.m.

I failed at my one job. I couldn't reach Sheriff Delacruz. I was scared to leave an explicit message. What if the dispatcher was one of the bad guys? Hell, what if Delacruz was? The dispatcher finally took pity on an LOL, my term for little old lady, and told me Delacruz was in Olympia for a two-day conference with other state sheriffs. Budget cuts and such. He'd be back tomorrow afternoon. If I wouldn't leave a message, I'd have to wait until then.

I'm old enough to be pretty good at waiting. It's one of the things that improves with age. But not so much this time. Setting aside concerns for Bear and myself, I was in a panic for Deputy Keegan. I felt all fluttery. To make matters worse, I heard voices coming from Jessica's office. Loud voices. Rachael yelling. Ben pleading. Were they talking about BB? What was that about?

Luckily, Bear arrived before long. New worry lines were etched into the wrinkles on his old face. I told him that I couldn't reach Delacruz as we limped together into Frankie's room.

Frankie poo-pooed my concern about the sheriff. He said, "Ez okay, Miss Lily. Mi famiglia stronger than the sheriff and all the deputies. We do not need them to end this evil." Of course he wouldn't want them around, what with them being law enforcement and him being law disturbance and all.

"Keegan's in the woods at that makeshift studio. I'm sure of it," Bear

said. *"If the bastards got ahead of this storm they flew her in by he-licopter. Like they did with Solana."* His voice sounded tight, each word clipped short.

Vinny replied he had left a message for Ghost to go locate the studio. *"Nobody knows these woods like this man who lives in them. We have helicopters, too. We wait for word from Ghost, then we go."*

"How did you leave a message?" Bear indicated the rain pelting Frankie's patio door.

"Sat phone. When Ghost finds this movie place, he call."

Bear frowned. Neither of us knows satellite from Shinola. *"Will it work in this weather?"*

Vinny nodded. *"Ghost powers with solar battery when the weather allows."*

Bear turned to Frankie, nearly pleading. *"You need to get a strike team in there first, before releasing the full force. Get Keegan out first, otherwise ..."* His sentence died before it finished its thought.

"Otherwise they'll rape her and beat her and murder her in front of a goddamn camera," I screamed inside my head.

Then the capo became The Capo. Frankie made it clear that he would end the movie making ASAP. We were not to worry about that. But! His goal was to put the gang behind it out of the entertainment business. Keegan was not his priority. *"If we can save this lady officer we will. If not ..."* he shrugged.

Bear's face got as dark as the storm clouds that were dumping buckets. *"If you just bust in there, they may kill her. You need to get her out first. We know the building plan from Solana's description. A team – "*

Frankie stopped him. *"– As I say, we do what we can."* Icicles dripped from his vocal chords. *"I have spoken, Signore Bear."* And that ended that. He waved a dismissive hand, indicating Vinny should open the door and usher us out.

Bear and Frankie glowered at each other as Bear stood, leaning ahead on his cane, his chin shoved forward. You'd think it was a college locker room from the testosterone level, not two broken old men rattling sabers.

I saw Vinny glance from his boss to Bear then to me. He raised an eyebrow, which was a passion play of emotion from Mr. Stone Face. He must be as upset as I was. Bear and Frankie just had to keep working as allies.

As we left the room, Vinny whispered in my ear, "Tell Signore Bear I will alert Ghost of this need to save his Cupcake person."

- Lily Gilbert, Secretive Assistant to PI Bear Jacobs

Nausea woke Keegan. She opened her eyes enough to roll off her back and vomit onto a hard, cold floor. Then she wiped her mouth on the hem of her t-shirt. Her shoulders ached. The back of her head, too.

What did I ...?

Her brain began to clear.

My hands are free.

She sat up causing her head to spin and squeezed her eyes shut until the vertigo passed. Then she opened them and gingerly looked around. Cement block walls. Between them and her, bars. Not thick like a cell. More like a cage. She was in a kennel big enough for a Rottweiler or a Great Dane. Bars above her allowed her room to sit up but not stand up. She couldn't have stood at the moment anyway, not the way the room continued to revolve.

That girl. What was her name? Solana. Solana had been in this place.

A weapon. She needed a weapon. She thought about it, her brain laboring to reconstruct. No gun. Rita had it. No cell phone. It was in the pocket of her hoodie, the one she'd removed in the sunny meadow at the homeless camp. Nothing in her pockets. Then she felt the ten-penny nail stuck into the button hole of her jeans above the zipper.

She'd been hammering. *Yeah, that's right.* A bench. Making it. Nails between her teeth, like any carpenter on the job. She'd grabbed one when the hand pushed her down from behind. Clutched it in her hand. Jabbed it into the buttonhole when her hands were in the dirt under her stomach. Hid it there before the bastards tied her arms behind her back.

A goddamn nail. Not much by way of weaponry. But something.

Help me.

For the first time in a long time, Keegan felt close to tears. She was scared, but she was sure of one thing. Her partner. If she couldn't save herself, he would. Clay Galligan would find her.

✦ ✦ ✦

After they were evicted from Frankie's room by Vinny, Lily and Bear were alone in the hall.

"What did he say to you?" Bear growled.

Lily paraphrased. "Vinny said to tell you he would alert Ghost to Keegan. That she needs to be evacuated before *la famiglia* attacks."

"Good," Bear nodded. "Tolerable." He blew out a big breath. "Lily, I want to kill Clay. For doing this. Whether Keegan dies or not. Whether he comes after us or not."

"Oh, Bear. We're not sure. Just because you saw a photo of him and the Ape doesn't mean that – "

Bear cut her off. "It makes sense. The pieces all fit. I even left him fucking messages every step of the way. He knew we were in that bar. He knew what we might find, that we were getting close."

"But how could he do this?"

"I know you gals lust after his ass. I want to *own* it." Then he turned and *kachunked* down the hall toward his room, his quad cane thudding the floor like a bass drumstick.

"Bear, I – " Lily called after him then thought better of it. If he needed time alone until they heard from Ghost, so be it. Moments later, Charlie wheeled out of the room like a pheasant flushed from a fence line.

"What the fuck is up with Bear? He just told me to get out. All I did was ask him how his afternoon went." Charlie's higher-than-average voice reached new heights.

Lily patted his scrawny forearm. "Come on, Charlie. Eunice is in the living room. Let's talk there."

Eunice was making earrings. The game table was covered with clear plastic containers of backings, hooks, colorful beads, crystals, and tiny semi-precious stones. When Lily and Charlie rolled in, Eunice was whistling along with the canaries. She had a light beam on a headband around her spiked orange hair and was snipping a bit of gold wire with needle nose pliers.

"Oh Lily!" she said, looking up. "These are for Alita. She's such a sweet girl. What do you think?"

Lily eyed the three inch Technicolor strands, each ending with clusters of petite heart charms. If Eunice could figure how to add strobe lights, she probably would. "She'll love them, Eunice."

"And these are for you!"

"Oh!" Lily exclaimed at the beaded hoops. "They're so, ah, big. Must have taken forever." Gamely, she began to attach the heavy circles to her ears.

"Keep away from me with that stuff," Charlie sniped as Eunice began to eye him.

"Oh, but I thought rings for the men," Eunice said, her eyebrows lifting in a V of disappointment. She held up a strand of dark brown sparklies on a curl of wire that could wrap around a finger multiple times. "I've used my dullest gems and stones. Very manly."

"Maybe. But I'm not manly enough to wear one."

Furball strolled into the room and looked around. The canaries stopped their whistling. Having accomplished that mission, the big orange cat leapt onto Charlie's lap and draped himself across those boney knees. Charlie obligingly moved away from the stormy windows closer to the gas fireplace, next to Lily. "Now, tell us what's going on."

While Lily brought them up to speed, Bear came into the room. He took a seat in a chair wide enough for a man of ample backside. "Sorry," he muttered to Charlie.

They all knew it was a major statement of repentance from the big man. Lily the Peacemaker said, "It's a hard time, Bear. We're all worried about Deputy Keegan, aren't we Charlie?"

"Absolutely. Nice looking gal like that." Charlie fancied himself a lady's man although Lily couldn't image why.

"I'll make her some lovely chandelier drop earrings for when she gets back," Eunice chirped.

Bear simply stared at her. Then he turned to Lily and said, "Vinny just called. Said he'd heard from Ghost that he already knows where that studio is. Found it after he brought Solana to us. He was just curious, I guess. Doesn't want unknowns in his woods."

"What is this place?" Charlie asked. "What kind of building exists back in the woods?"

"Ghost says it looks like an old storehouse or barn. One maybe used by loggers back in the day."

"Why would loggers need a barn?"

"Keep equipment dry, stable work horses, run a kitchen, a bunkhouse ... shit, Charlie, I don't know. But it's there."

"So Frankie will send in the cavalry?" Lily asked.

"In the morning. If the weather lets up."

"Surely they won't have had time to do anything to the deputy. I mean, make a film. I mean ..." Charlie closed his mouth, lips puckered in disgust.

"Ghost is going in for her before daybreak."

"All on his own?"

"He told Vinny he prefers it that way. He'll do it before Frankie's troops can get there by copter."

"How will we know when she's okay?" Eunice asked, a small tuft of beads becoming a dragonfly in her clever hands.

"He'll call Vinny if, I mean when, he gets her out. We'll meet them at the same meadow where I talked to Ghost after he saved Solana. The one Vinny took me to." He held up a hand. "And no need to worry about me, Lily. If Keegan gets that far, I should be safe from Clay. He might be dead by then."

Lily knew exactly what she needed to do. She stretched her back, yawned and unlocked the brakes on her wheelchair. "Guess I'll hit the hay for now then. Nothing more til morning." Night, everyone." She wheeled to her room and rang for help getting ready for bed. She already knew the person on duty was her favorite aide.

While she waited for Chrissie, she removed the hoop earrings which were surely stretching her old earlobes down to her shoulder blades.

✦   ✦   ✦

Ben sat across the desk from Jessica in her office. They'd been reviewing a leasing contract for a larger commercial dishwasher. Jessica often consulted him on the day-to-day business details.

Ben's daughter, Rachael, had stomped in moments before, neatly plopping BB into Ben's lap. The odor of sour baby wafted into the room with them.

Jessica had leaned back in her chair, quiet as a statue. She was not an active participant in this confrontation, merely the audience. It was a scene that she thought was all too commonplace in this day and age of grandparents raising grandchildren. She saw no graceful way to escape the room unnoticed, so she settled for witness to the drama. Actually, she'd been waiting for something like this to happen.

What will Ben do?

"He doesn't even like me, Dad," Rachael said, pleading with her father from the other guest chair.

"Nonsense," Ben answered cuddling the fractious Baby Boy against his chest. The baby settled down to a watery coo.

"And I don't like him. All the noise, the mess." Her arms were akimbo over her chest, her lovely young face splotched with anger. Or sorrow. Jessica couldn't tell which.

"He's a *baby*, honey. What do you expect?" Ben the Reasonable.

"Not him. I can't do it. I won't. If you won't keep him, I need to give him to whoever takes in babies. Run an ad. Find better parents than me."

Jessica knew what was on Ben's face. A terrible disbelief of what he was hearing. She'd felt that kind of incredulity herself when they'd told her that her husband was dead. But Ben was doing everything he could to maintain his composure. "Rachael, we can work this out. The situation isn't hopeless. What about his father? We've never talked about him. How about I go to him, see what he wants."

"No, you can't, Dad. BB's father? Who the hell even knows where the shithead is?" Rachael broke down. She bent at the waist, held her face in her hands. Through her snot and tears, she mourned, "I don't even know for sure *who* he is."

"Rachael," Ben cajoled. "You've been down before. You've come back from the brink every time."

"Not like this. Never like this. I'll never want this mommy life. Swear to God."

Conversation stopped for a long, long time other than Rachael's gulps and sighs and BB's fussing. Ben finally stood and handed the baby to a very startled Jessica. He turned to his daughter who looked like a torn rag-doll limp in her chair.

"Rachael," he said. Jessica and Rachael both looked up. This voice came from a different Ben. This was a hard voice, uncompromising and cold, from a man known for calm. "If you leave this baby ... if you run now ... this is it. I don't want you to come back. Not ever. No more money for drugs and booze. No more bail in the middle of the night. No more little girl lost. No more."

Ben left the room. Jessica, holding the baby, had to decide. She could go to Grandpa Ben with BB. Or she could give the child back to his mother. Her choice was so very sad. But it was so very simple for her to make.

✦ ✦ ✦

Sylvia's date was for the coming Saturday night. Vinny Tononi. Hunk. Man of mystery. Of a certain sort of ... experience, shall we say.

She planned to meet him at Latin's Ranch. Sylvia didn't feel right having him come to her home. Not yet. Not with that invisible blinking sign over the door that screamed, *I'm the only one here. Come on in, big boy, and play me like a harp.*

She opened her closet and stood back to take inventory. Organized by season. Then by color. White, white, white, beige, beige, beige, dove, dove, dove, etc, etc, etc. Sylvia sighed. No heart-stopping red, bluesy blue, smoking silver. Nothing sexy except, and here she looked down to the bottom of her closet, smiled and picked up a box. She put it on her bed and opened it, lifting out the treasure. Stilettos. Strappy, sassy, made to make the wearer shudder with pain and the observer shudder with passion. Sylvia dangled one in front of Kyle's photo and said, "Your friend Tony calls them come-fuck-me shoes." She beamed at the torturous footwear and nearly purred. Sylvia had a shoe thing. It was an addiction she truly kept in the closet. "Well, yes, you're right, Kyle. Hardly appropriate for a movie." Sighing again, she returned the sassy little numbers to their box and moved on to the shelf of loafers.

At last, she admitted defeat. "I'm not the type of woman who has the type of wardrobe worn for the type of man that Vinny must be." Sylvia wore wools and silks, not the spandex and feather boas she imagined from too many episodes of *The Sopranos*. "He'll just have to accept what I choose to wear, and that's all there is to it."

Kyle didn't disagree. But if the cherished man in the photo could have smiled, it would have stretched ear to ear as Sylvia went to her drawer and once again pulled out the sexy raspberry underwear.

✦　✦　✦

Ghost watched.

Life in the woods had made his sight acute in the darkness of old growth forest or starless nights. His other senses were also heightened as is said of a blind man. He heard the owl hunting before dawn, smelled the fear of its kill.

Now he watched the old barn of a building. From the outside it was a derelict, long forgotten deep in national forest territory and settling under the weight of moss and moisture. Hard to reach, far from hiking trails and prying eyes. A now overgrown track had led to it at one time although eyes less trained than his would never have picked it out. Only a small patch near it had been cleared for a helicopter to land. One was there now.

If movies were being made with digital cameras and casts of characters, Ghost could see no sign of it from the outside. But the big three-bay door was open. He assumed it was the one Solana had used to make her escape. No wonder she had thought of this place as a warehouse or hangar.

It was not yet daylight. Ghost had seen nothing since two men came outside to smoke. Two tired men awake in the night. The only watchmen he'd seen. The place was poorly guarded, but why should it need any better, out here in the middle of nowhere?

Ghost had no way of knowing how many had come in the helicopter. Two guards were nothing, but he must be cautious. He heard and saw no motion, no conversation. Stealthy as a cougar on the hunt, he approached the enormous doorway.

Solana had told him she'd crept along a dark wall before running outside. There was a wardrobe room where she had hidden and before that, the room with the cages. His plan was to backtrack along the same path. Unlike Solana, he was armed. Well armed. He even carried an extra gun for the woman cop when he found her. A Springfield pistol with a 17 shot clip. A cop should know what to do with it.

Wild rhodies and salal bushes provided the cover Ghost needed to reach the entrance. His back against the rough exterior of the building, he slowly peered into the darkness within. Nothing but outlines of klieg lights and other film equipment. And one of the guards asleep in a director's chair, body sprawled, head back and snoring softly.

It would be an easy throat to cut. But not yet. If the other guard found this one dead, he'd raise the alarm. Ghost's smile to himself was cold as a statue's.

I'll do them both if that happens. Something to look forward to.

The wild man slipped inside the bay door and edged his way along the wall. Solana's description of the place had been good. He moved toward a doorway and slithered inside. It must be the wardrobe room. He stopped and listened. Nothing but the snoring from the sleeping guard. Ghost exited the room still following the wall through the darkness. He could see another doorway dead ahead. Light was spilling from the room. Along with voices.

Before he got close enough to hear what they said, a voice behind him commanded, "Stop right there."

Long before that command was fully issued, Ghost swung around, assessed the size of the man behind him and plunged the knife he'd been holding deep between the large ribs that encircle the lungs.

✦ ✦ ✦

Keegan heard footsteps approach. She tensed and positioned the ten-penny nail in her hand, between her fingers pointing outward. She gathered herself into a crouch position. The cage might not allow her to stand, but if someone opened its door she could spring at them.

She waited, watching the doorway, glad the other cages were empty. When she saw the first man enter the room, she exhaled. The adrenalin in her body began to drain as she relaxed. "Clay!" she said shakily. "'Bout time you stopped by, partner." She heard the relief in her own voice. She feared she would cry right there in front of him. Clay would save her.

Keegan's joy was short lived. She saw the man behind Clay and she tensed again. "Who? ... isn't that? ..."

"Always the detective, aren't you, Keegan? Better than the rest of us. Yeah, that's Joey the Ape. Control between the gang and me." Clay made no move toward letting her out of the padlocked cage. Instead, he just grinned.

"Unlock the door, Clay. Hurry! There are at least two other guards here. We need to –"

"Shut up, you stupid bitch, and *detect*. They're with me. I'm with them. Have been for years. And you are about to star as a lady cop getting her just desserts. A short film but oh so sweet to a shitload of buyers."

Keegan's mind reeled. Her heart raced. She thought she might pass out. "Clay, what are you doing?"

"I've been undercover for *my* gang for a long, long time. And you, you idiot, thought I couldn't play a role. You and that crippled old bastard you admire so much." He leaned closer and leered. "You never guessed, did you, Jo? Always thought I was a good little sidekick, following you around, learning from the wise. Well, suck my dick, sweetheart." He stood up and said to the Ape, "Get her out of that cage and bring her out for her debut. I'll enjoy watching the filming of this one myself. Or should I say, 'the shooting'?" He laughed and left the room.

Keegan's world collapsed. Her partner, her friend, her trust. Gone. But still, she readied herself again. Her body knew what to do even though her mind was reeling.

"I'm gonna love this," the Ape said, making a show of choosing the right key. Slowly, he approached the padlock and inserted the key. At the exact second he removed the lock from the cage, three things happened.

A gun blast ricocheted around the studio walls.

Joey the Ape turned toward the sound.

Keegan leapt at him, sinking the nail into the soft tissue of his neck.

A gasp bubbled from the Ape's mouth as he sunk to his knees, grabbing for his throat. Keegan watched, now out of confinement and leaning against a wall. Her body wobbled until her muscles caught up with the adrenalin flooding her system once more.

Too much time in a cage.

Without warning, a wild man was in front of her. He looked at the Ape. "A nail?" he said with wonder in his voice. Then he drew his knife across Ape's throat to finish the job. "For Solana," he said as he wiped the blade on the dead man's shirt.

Next he turned to Keegan and, wedging a gun into her hand, demanded, "Follow me. Now."

She didn't question. She moved behind him, flying fast and low out of the room and into the studio. Along the back wall, she tripped over the body of an unknown man. *Blood.* She caught her balance and continued after the wild man while she pulled the slide and chambered a round in the gun he had given her. Keegan vowed she would not be captured again.

Shots blasted through the studio, one hitting the wall just ahead of her. It was so dark. She fired back, and more shots came. She heard the wild man grunt, but he continued running.

Clay screamed, "Stop there! Leave her and I'll let you live."

Her rescuer never faltered. Together, they tore out through the enormous bay door and disappeared into the salal under the looming firs that enfolded them in darkness.

Keegan heard the wild man screaming into a phone, "We're out." Then from behind her, Clay shouting, 'After them!' Next, the whoop whoop whoop of a helicopter lowering itself toward land. After that, the blood pounding in her ears masked everything else.

Run.

She couldn't guess how far they'd gone as they dodged their way through the undergrowth.

Broken field running.

When they stopped she noticed that her bare arms were slashed by blackberry vines.

Looks like I lost a cat fight.

The wild man breathed into her ear, "They're the good guys in the helicopter. But we couldn't wait for them. Your partner and two others are following us."

"You're Ghost, aren't you?" She asked. The one who'd rescued Solana. Who else could this feral savior be?

Under his facial camo she saw a brief hint of softness around his mouth. "You're smart. For a cop."

"You've been hit," she said, seeing the blood oozing through his sleeve and down his arm. "Let me bind that."

"No time now." Then he turned and ran once more.

Keegan, used to giving the orders, bristled. But she knew he outclassed her in the woods. She needed to listen to him. Her insides felt physically bruised by Clay's betrayal, but the ache was nothing compared to the wave of rage that threatened to overpower her. She had trusted him, counted on him, shared secrets with him. Not once had she questioned his loyalty. And she'd been wrong. Conned, played. What kind of an investigator was she?

She had to control this fury. She had to listen to Ghost because at this moment, her need for help was greater than her need for revenge. She followed the wild man deeper into the forest.

CHAPTER ELEVEN

Case Notes
September 21, 10 a.m.

Everyone was up early. I couldn't finish Aurora's banana waffle no matter how yummy it was. Too many butterflies. Speaking of insects, I couldn't help but notice the enormous beaded dragonfly that held Aurora's salt and pepper locks to the back of her head. I admit it looked kind of pretty. But after one of my new hoop earrings latched onto my collar button for the third time, I vowed to snatch them off the instant I was out of Eunice's sight.

I pushed my plate in front of Bear. "Finish that. Then come outside with me. We're just about ready."

"We? Ready?"

"Oh, give it a rest. You need back-up and you're going to get it. Besides, it's for Keegan, not for you."

He crammed the rest of the waffle into his face and stood. "Leth go outhide then." He headed for the backdoor through the kitchen.

"Not that way. Out front." I led the way. As we moved through the living room to the front door, I explained. "If – when – Ghost and Keegan get to you and Vinny out there where you're supposed to meet, one of them may be in bad shape. Or both of them. Neither of you two have medical training. But Chrissie does. So I talked to her last night."

I opened the front door and ushered Bear through. He'd probably

slept poorly. I thought he leaned more heavily on his cane than usu-
al. I'm sure he's blaming himself for not seeing that Clay was the
connection between the mobs and the movies. Nothing will keep
you awake like self recrimination.

- Lily Gilbert, Determined Assistant to PI Bear Jacobs

The storm had passed, but the morning sun was still too weak to warm old bones. Bear felt a shiver of cold as he stood on the porch next to Lily. Or a shiver of something. He'd been experiencing entirely too many god-damn emotions in the past twelve hours, and it had to stop. It was time for sense not sentiment.

He looked down the steps at Vinny's Caddy in the driveway ahead of them. Next to it was Sam's Silverado. "What's going on, Lily?"

"We're turning the Caddy into a makeshift ambulance," Lily explained. Chrissie, closely supervised by Vinny, was loading a cardboard box into the back seat of his beloved car. "Chrissie's gathered bandages, sterile pads, disinfectants, antiseptic, pain relievers, blankets, all that stuff. Triage if Ghost or Keegan need it. And the backseat is plenty big enough for one of them to be prone."

Lily turned from the scene in front of them to look at Bear. "Chrissie and I will follow you with Sam in his truck. If Keegan and Ghost are both wounded, the truck's back seat works for one of them, and I know enough about nursing care to lend a hand. And Bear? Remember that Sam has Winnie. I mean just in case."

Bear looked at Lily. He saw a slender woman with a puff of hair, soft as a dandelion gone to seed. Her lovely skin was as supple as a favorite chamois cloth. He could see from her determined frown that she was prepared for yet another lecture about her safety. But he didn't want to lecture her. Instead, he wanted to tell her how life had meaning when she was around.

More of these goddamn emotions, goddamn it.

Bear nodded at his eWatson and said, "Very good, Lily. Very well done. Now we just wait for the call from Ghost."

✦   ✦   ✦

A fallen fir was the nurse log for a stand of new seedlings. Ghost slid down onto the mossy trunk and leaned against a couple of the young trees, dropping the pack and gun he carried. Everything was still damp from the night's rain. The footing was been slick but the early morning light had allowed them to pull far ahead of their followers.

Keegan, gulping in air after the long hard run, could see a pallor growing under the camouflage paint on the wild man's face. "You're losing too much blood. I have to patch that shoulder."

"Yes. They'll start tracking us by the blood I'm leaving behind. But be quick."

She helped him unbutton the old military jacket. It was in tatters, stained with months of life in the rough. Now a bullet had passed through his shoulder and the jacket was seeping red. Keegan hoped it went through clean but couldn't really tell whether it had broken the collar bone on its way.

"Gather some of those fir needles and pack them around the wound," Ghost said. "Use some pitch if you can get to it."

Keegan complied, figuring he knew more about living in the woods than she did. As she gathered the needles and pitch he told her, "The oil disinfects and the pitch is sticky enough to help the wound start to close. Like it does for the tree when it gets a wound."

He removed his undershirt. She ripped it in half, placed the fir products on the entrance and exit wounds, then bound everything in place by tying the two halves of the shirt together. Next she removed her own t-shirt revealing the sports bra beneath. "Might as well get berry scratches on my gut, too," she muttered as she applied her shirt above his. "Best I can do 'til we get where I can wash that wound."

As she worked, Ghost told her what had happened in the studio. When Ghost knifed the guard, the man's gun had gone off. Clay was already in the studio. He'd missed Ghost huddled against the dark back wall when he left the room where Keegan was captive. When Ghost slipped into the room of cages, Keegan was wielding a nail against the Ape.

"Where'd it come from?" Ghost asked, and Keegan explained how she happened to have a carpenter's nail.

"Well done," Ghost said and Keegan was inordinately pleased by his approval. "Clay rounded up a couple guys to come find where the shot went off. He spotted us when we headed for the garage door. And the fireworks began." The whole thing had taken a matter of seconds.

Keegan finished the makeshift patchwork to his shoulder, and Ghost handed her the SAT phone. "Call your friend. The old man that Vinny calls Bear. Tell him we're over an hour from the meeting place."

"Bear's behind this?"

Ghost took a moment to answer while he picked up the pack and his gun. "Let's say he's the only one you should ask about."

She cocked her head, shrugged and began to key in the number.

"Lean forward," Ghost said.

She did.

He reached out.

For one crazy second, she thought this wounded man was going to feel her up with his one good hand. Instead he brushed fingers across her chest with the force of a whisk broom. "Wolf spider. They can bite bad. It's gone now."

Jesus. My hero. Twice in one fucking day.

✦ ✦ ✦

When Jessica came down for breakfast, the residents were long gone. Ben was alone in the dining room with BB. He was holding a bottle and mumbling some language that Jessica figured was Grandparent-Speak. In fact, she'd heard all the residents use it with BB from time to time.

She went to the kitchen and came back with dry toast and black coffee, having ignored Aurora's mutterings about proper breakfasts. She pulled out a chair and sat next to Ben. He reached over and kissed her cheek, then handed her a note scrawled on a sheet of yellow notebook paper. "Found this when I got BB up. It was in his crib next to him." He looked back to the baby and said, "Whosa boy, whosa grampa boy, is 'e oo? Is 'e oo?"

Jessica read:

"Can't do it. Call me a creep if you want. BB is yours. Give him away or keep him. Do what you want. If you keep him, good luck with a name."

She read it again, folded it, and put it on the tabletop next to Ben's coffee mug. She took a sip of her own brew but ignored her toast. Maybe if it had butter or jam. She waited for him to speak.

"You didn't sign on for this, Jess. You don't need to raise this baby with me. We'll be going as soon as I can pack up his things." The hopeless tone of his voice said more than his words.

Jessica knew Ben had loved her for years, waiting for her to get over the death of her husband, waiting for her to recognize her love for him, waiting for her to commit. She couldn't commit, not as long as Rachael broke his heart with such frequency. But now? Maybe the last great tear had been ripped through that kind heart of his. Maybe now it could truly mend. The needs of his grandson might just overshadow the needs of his daughter and save Ben from the destruction that Rachael was choosing for herself. Now, at last, Jessica felt she could truly act.

"Ben Stassen, will you marry me?"

✦   ✦   ✦

They waited in a group at the Caddy and the Silverado, parked and ready in front of Latin's Ranch. There'd been no contact since Ghost's call to Vinny before daylight, "We're out." Now the sun was beginning to tame the dampness in the air. Next it would work its magic on the mud. Snakes of steam rose from the fields.

They waited.

When the call finally came, Bear yelped into the phone. "Ghost?"

Vinny, Chrissie, Lily and Sam nearly held their breath in unison.

"No, Bear, it's Keegan."

"Keegan! You're free?" He turned to the group and nodded when she answered. The whole group exhaled. Lily and Sam high-fived. Chrissie tried to do the same with Vinny, but he looked startled by the gesture. And everyone knew you never, never startled Vinny.

"Yes, I'm with Ghost." Static interfered. And Keegan was whispering. Bear strained to hear. "We're running from Clay and at least one other. Maybe two. Ghost is hurt pretty bad. He says we're an hour or more from your meet spot."

"We'll be there."

Her voice faltered. "You know about Clay, right?"

"Yes, Jo, we know. We'll get you out before Clay gets to you. That's a promise."

"Careful what you promise, Bear. Ghost is bleeding bad. We're moving slow now."

"One of my few beliefs is that you can do anything. Now haul ass, Cupcake."

"Sweet talker." The line went dead.

If asked, Bear would have denied tears as he told the others the news. They were getting close, but Ghost was wounded. The posse leaped into action, buckled up and galloped away in their metallic steeds. The Silverado followed the Caddy to the woodland meadow where Vinny and Bear had met Ghost before, less than a week ago.

"When will Frankie's 'copter be in the air?" Bear asked as they started the journey. Vinny had been having his own phone conversations throughout the morning hours, and Bear hoped for an update.

"*Signore* Bear. It was over the building when Ghost called early. Waiting for that. It has landed. My team finds the studio and four men, two dead when they arrive. The one with the nail in his neck and the slash across the throat? He is Joey the Ape."

A nail?

"Ghost and your Cupcake are gone when they get there. No other victims in cages. This is a good thing."

"Hmm. They may make films in batches. That would make sense. Capturing Keegan got them out of sync."

"The enemy helicopter that we found there? It has disappeared." Vinny's cold eyes momentarily sparkled as he glanced at Bear. "And our *Padrone* has another flying bird to add to his fleet."

"Ah. And what about the rest? Movie equipment and stuff?"

"It burns when the building burns."

Mob justice. No evidence left. Remind me never to cross these guys.

"About the living guys you found there?" Bear dared to ask. "Where are they?"

Vinny drove silently for a few moments. "This you do not want to know."

All righty.

Bear looked back over his shoulder. Sam's Silverado followed behind, punching an even larger hole through the overgrowth than the Caddy made. Cedar branches slapped the hood, clinging to the mirrors and wipers.

Once they arrived at their destination, it took no small amount of maneuvering for Vinny and Sam to turn both behemoths around. It looked like a slow motion square dance. They do-si-doed beside the meadow until they aimed back down the trail for a quick exit. The little rescue team stood next to the cars once again, anxiously waiting for Keegan and Ghost. Those who could stamped their feet in the cold. Chrissie passed around a Thermos of hot coffee. Bear heard Vinny chamber a round and do whatever else was needed by special weaponry. They were too nervous to talk until they heard a distant sound, shrill and multi-leveled and hair-raising.

"Wolves?" Bear asked, breaking their silence.

"Banshees?" Lily asked.

"Fuck!" said Sam, much to Bear's surprise. Sam didn't talk like that when ladies were around. "Dogs. That goddamn feral pack nearly killed Latin Dancer." Sam spit on the ground then went to his Silverado, opened the diamond plate tool box in the truck bed, and removed Winnie. "Don't like to kill a dog. But some in that pack are rabid. Virus gets to their brains. They die in pain. And they cause a lot of pain along the way."

Bear listened as the distant howling and yipping became more distinct. "Sounds like they're looking for a kill. They probably denned up somewhere during the storm. Hungry now."

"Sam, are they coming this way?" Lily asked.

He cocked his head toward the racket then nodded. "Sounds it. They may smell blood."

"Is one of us bleeding?" Chrissie eyed each of them suspiciously.

"No, but Ghost is getting closer to us. Keegan said he's wounded," Bear said. "Vinny, why don't you and Sam go to opposite sides of the meadow. Shoot whatever or whoever you have to. We'll stay here with the cars so Keegan can see us."

"Si. But *Signore* Bear? This Chrissie girl. She is best shot here." Vinny had reason to know having seen her marksmanship in adventures past. "I give her rifle, too. And pistol to you."

Armed and ready, Sam, Vinny and Chrissie triangulated locations on the rim of the meadow. Each stepped into the woods for cover. They would act if Clay – or the dogs – arrived too soon for the team to spirit Ghost and Keegan away.

Bear handed his phone to Lily. "In case Keegan calls again, answer it, okay? I want to keep watch. Can't seem to manage both just now. Don't multitask like I used to." He rested one paw on his quad cane with the pistol in his other.

✦   ✦   ✦

Keegan wanted to cajole Ghost to hurry, but he was nearly done-in. He'd tried to make her go on without him, but that was out of the question. She was afraid he would pass out from blood loss. He'd been leaning heavily on her for the last half hour, and she was near exhaustion herself.

At one point they had gotten far enough ahead of their trackers that they could no longer hear them. But not now. Keegan stopped long enough to shoot half a clip into the woods behind them. She heard a yelp and thought she must have hit someone.

Hope it was Clay.

But she knew that even if she hit him, he'd never call off the hunt. Not as long as he was still standing. Clay was a tough partner. Now a tough adversary. Keegan strangled a cry that threatened to air the depth of her despair.

When she heard the howling, she thought it might be her own for one bizarre second. It sounded so much like she felt. She tried to identify it.

A wolf pack? In Washington? No way.

"I've heard them before. Dogs," Ghost said in a weakened voice. "Dangerous. I've seen them attack a coyote. They'll track my blood faster than the men can. Leave me. Do it."

"Shut up. Now move." Keegan hoped to sound harder assed than she felt.

✦   ✦   ✦

Bear saw motion through the trees. A large form pushing through. Branches waved and snapped.

Elk?

No ... two people, wobbling ... Ghost, arm around Keegan and hers around him. The two struggled from the darkness into the now bright meadow. Once in the clearing, they fell together. Bear saw nobody exit the woods directly behind them.

"Vinny! Chrissie!" Bear roared. "Help them. Sam, stay on watch."

Vinny got to the collapsed couple first. He bodily lifted Ghost over a shoulder with help from Chrissie when she arrived. As they staggered back across the meadow toward the Caddy, she was already trying to find a pulse.

Keegan arose and hobbled to Bear. He handed his gun and cane to Lily in time to encircle the deputy in his enormous arms. He tried to avoid the bloody slashes on her body and arms as she trembled against his chest. "Welcome home, Cupcake. Now let's get you into the Caddy."

Chrissie was already in the foot well on her knees. Ghost was sprawled on the backseat, and the aide was cutting free the t-shirt packing that Keegan had jerry-rigged. "Ugh! He needs blood, now," she yelled. "Vinny, we gotta move."

"I take them both to the doctor of the Sapienza *famiglia*," Vinny said. "He ask no questions about these wounds."

"Well hurry," Chrissie snapped.

Lily removed her shawl and wound it around Keegan then Bear nudged the exhausted deputy into the front seat.

"Sam, Lily and I will be right behind you."

Vinny hesitated. "You do not mean this. You will not get out before this bad cop comes. You need Vinny here."

"I need you to save Ghost. I can't drive. Neither can Lily. Has to be you. Now go."

"*Merda*," Vinny said, then disappeared into the Caddy and gunned it.

"You have no intention of leaving, do you?" Lily said to Bear as the big car disappeared into the woods. The two stood on their walker and cane while Sam and Winnie waited in the woods.

"It's like I told you, Lily. I want to kill Clay."

She handed back his gun, the pistol that Vinny had left him. "You know what you're doing, big man? You can live with this?"

"Some crimes can't wait for due process." Bear looked at her, searching for disapproval. He found none. "You should wait in the truck. You don't need to see this."

She shrugged. "Clay's a mad dog as surely as those in that pack. A cop we trusted turned rabid. Whatever his reason, he's hurt too many of us, endangered us. I'll stay right here until you're ready to go."

Before she finished the statement, Clay appeared on the other side of the meadow, exactly where Ghost and Keegan had materialized. Handsome still, although sodden from the wet forest and sagging from exhaustion. He was alone and seemed to be limping.

"Must be the others abandoned him if any were still with him. Or they're circling around behind us," Bear said. "If so, Sam will see them."

"Looks like blood on his pant leg," Lily muttered. "He's limping."

"Bear, you fuckin' has-been. You just couldn't leave it alone. Gonna be my pleasure to put you down like an old horse," Clay yelled from mid-meadow, gasping for air between words. "You, too, you crazy old bitch. Both of you should have been underground years ago. You've destroyed everything. But it's my turn now."

He raised his rifle to fire but seemed to falter from weakness or exhaustion. Then he turned toward the racket coming ever closer. With a terrible yowl, the first of the dogs burst into the meadow from the woods. Big and shaggy, more shepherd than anything else, but much larger. The hair on its neck stood straight up through clots of wet mud. It lowered its head and snarled through bared teeth. Bear could see foam bubbling around its muzzle.

The predator sprung forward, rushing toward Clay. Before the deputy could revise his aim from Bear to the dog, a shot brought the massive animal down.

Clay swung around to see Sam step out of the woods. "That was one that got to Latin Dancer. Did it for the colt, not you."

Other dogs dashed out of the woods, snarling and yapping. Clay fired, downing one before the rest spread out around him. A silent Doberman he did not see hit him first, grabbing the calf of his wounded leg.

Clay clubbed at it with the rifle, crying out, "Shoot it."

But no shot came. Another beast grabbed his wrist, and Clay fell. He screamed to Bear for help. Bear never raised his gun and held up a hand to stop Sam.

The fourth dog took the deputy's throat as two more began tearing meat from bone. Clay shrieked again and again but the animals were frenzied. Finally, the human sounds died under the blood lust.

Bear, Lily and Sam watched until the dogs took what shreds they wished and dragged them into the woods. Only then did Sam cross the meadow to join the other two. "If there's another man out there, he's long gone now," he observed. He raised his gun and put another shot into the dog Clay had hit, making sure it was out of any pain.

"I think we're done here." Bear took his time getting into Sam's truck, solicitous of Lily whose rosy cheeks had drained to an ivory pallor. There was no need to hurry now. The three shared the bench seat, all of them silenced by their own thoughts. Bear was glad they were near enough each other to touch.

As the truck bounced down the trail, Bear gave a thought to the mob's operation and the lack of evidence where a movie studio had once been. Now Clay was gone, with no clear evidence of his involvement or his death. A cop ripped apart by feral dogs.

Maybe I'm not so different from Frankie after all.

CHAPTER TWELVE

Case Notes
September 21, 9 p.m.

I'm beat tonight, so tired my eyes can't focus on my screen. It looks as gauzy as an old Doris Day movie. But so much has happened today, I want to get it all down before I forget. For an adult care home, you'd think it would be a lot snoozier at Latin's Ranch. The only one around here that relaxes all the time is Furball.
Sam, Bear and I got back home before Chrissie, Vinny and Ghost. We were able to tell the others what had happened out there in the meadow. Well, as much about it as they need to know. Not sure a graphic report of evisceration by canine is in anyone's best interest.
Turned out Frankie had been busy, too. He'd asked Jessica if there was room for Ghost to recover here after the doctor patches him up. The cost would be no issue. He said her feathers ruffled about housing another associate of his, indicating that she wasn't running a care center for gangsters. But when he told her that Ghost had saved Deputy Keegan's life, Jessica turned happy to help.
Funny thing ... Rachael has just moved out. So, yes, a room was available. Vinny delivered Ghost with Chrissie sticking to her patient like a Band-Aid. She'll be administering his antibiotics and changing the bandages and overall fussing under the guidance of the mobster medicine man. I can just imagine how a wild man like Ghost will like that. Could be the most traumatic thing he's faced yet.

Now, hold the bus. I want to go back to that 'Rachael-has- just-moved-out' thing. While we were trekking out to the meet in the woods, Ben Stassen was having a crisis of his own. Rachael apparently disappeared back to the street life. Left a note in BB's crib and vamoosed in the wee hours. I guess if you don't have an addictive personality yourself, it is impossible to understand why a person would choose to do that. Maybe I shouldn't think of it as a choice so much as a compulsion. Must feel like being a marionette at the mercy of some unknown handler who dances you closer and closer to the edge. Sounds melodramatic, I know. But the fact is, Rachael needs the street life so badly she's left Baby Boy behind. A baby already damaged by her lifestyle. He's too much for her, and she's left the future of this troubled little person up to Ben.

As it turns out, that's not a bad thing. Jessica and Ben are getting married. They're just beginning to make their plans, of course, but for sure those plans include raising the little one. Now that Jess is convinced Rachael is out of the picture, she's been kitchee-cooing as much as the rest of us. She's already asked me to be her matron of honor. Eunice wants the flower girl role. What fun it will be to plan a wedding.

Baby Boy not only gets a new Mommy and Daddy, he gets Uncles Bear, Charlie and Frankie, plus Aunts Eunice and Lily! And, drum roll please, an honest to goodness name of his own. Personally, I'm hoping they go with Baby Benny. Grandpa Bennett isn't committing yet. Eunice has offered to sponsor a Name Game, but since Bono and Eminem would in all fairness have to be on the list as Rachael's choices, I think Ben and Jessica need to choose this one on their own.

Also in the happy dance department, a call for me came in while I was gone. I returned it to find that Medicare has approved the cost of a prosthesis. So I have an appointment with a specialist for a final review and fitting. I'm going to walk again!

None of us saw Keegan tonight. I'm sure the famiglia *doctor patched her up a bit, at least physically. Some of those thorn scratches looked deep to me. I suppose she went home after that. And, of course, I'm sure she needs to meet with Sheriff Delacruz about made-to-order snuff films and the department's missing bastard, Deputy Clay Galligan. Wonder how many unsolved mysteries or blown investigations under Delacruz's command might lead right back to that one dirty officer?*

I must say Clay was a brilliant con man. We may never know why he decided on the path he took, but he was good at it. How could we all be so blind to what now seems so obvious? Makes me feel sheepish to know how long he had us fooled. It must be hitting Deputy Josephine Keegan seriously hard.

She is a fine officer and even finer human being. She has been kidnapped and terrorized by the one person she should be able to trust above all others. Clay Galligan has wounded her deeply, more than all those superficial scratches. Something like that can destroy your belief in yourself, make you question your own judgment and competence. How can a cop function that way? If you ask me, Jo's healing may take a long, long time.

- Lily Gilbert, Exhausted Assistant to PI Bear Jacobs

Bear believed Frankie owed them some explanations. At breakfast over fresh fruit cups and *huevos Benedictos*, the big man cleared his throat in a rumble that got everyone's attention. Then he said, "Talk to us, Frankie."

Frankie cut his eyes around the table. Lily, Charlie, Bear and his little dove, Eunice. The staff was too busy to pay much attention to their breakfast chitchat; they used the time to tidy resident rooms, glad to have the occupants out of the way. "This place, ez not for private talk," Frankie cautioned. When he reached for his tea cup, Bear noticed the beaded ring that spiraled around his index finger, from knuckle to sparkling knuckle.

"Oh, horseshit," Bear snorted. "There's not a mobster in the state who doesn't know where you are by now."

Frankie frowned but nodded. "Yes. My residence ez now known."

"If you want to stay here with us, you need to treat us like we matter. Right?" Bear looked at his gang of operatives.

"Absolutely," said the one who was soon to receive a new leg.

"Well, um, I guess. I mean if you want to," said the one whose nuts were sore most of the time.

"Without a doubt you must trust us," said the little dove with the spiky orange hair. "And furthermore, my sweet. If you ever again think my friend Lily doesn't belong in conversations with the men folk, I will hit you with my craft bag."

Frankie busied himself with a slow sip of hot tea. He dabbed his lips with his napkin. "I tell you this. Soon there ez nothing left. No evidence. No bad guys to be found. And no more of these films." His cleanup detail was doing just that: cleaning up all the dirty odds and ends.

Bear realized that Frankie had never used the actual name of the rival gang as he talked. He didn't call them Latin or Asian or Russian. He didn't mention whether they were under the thumb of the Black Hand when it came to profits. But as he talked, it was clear that if any gang felt they could muscle in on the established families, Frankie Sapienza had shown them otherwise.

"Frankie, one thing I don't get," Bear said. "Why a cop bar for a drop spot to pick up films? Because it would not be suspected? Because Clay could keep watch?"

"Si. And this bar? Ez only one such drop spot we now close." Frankie looked at Vinny and nodded.

Vinny looked at Bear and continued. "We also close a coffee stand with baristas that hand out DVDs to some buyers. And a pizza delivery. These places we find at the dark web place after we, ah, talk with the buyer from the bar. I do not know how this dark web works."

"I think I do," said Lily. "It's thousands of sites with tools to hide the addresses of their servers. The users bounce traffic from place to place around the globe, removing or adding layers of encryption. The sites are so hard to find that they've been used for drug sales and porn and even by whistleblowers. It shouldn't be mistaken with the so-called deep web ..."

At this point, Bear saw zoned out expressions all around the table. Lily must have noticed, too. She stopped. "Guess it isn't all that interesting to everyone."

It was time for the breakfast club to break up. Before it did, Bear said, "We know you may decide to move, Frankie. Or if you stay, there may be more security around here. Just so you know, we think of you as family. We'd like you to think of us as *famiglia*. We hope you stay." Bear had given this a lot of thought. In the end, he'd decided that having Frankie close at hand was more often helpful than having him off the ranch.

"We agree." All operatives, including one little dove, were of the same mind.

"But you'll have to talk to Jessica about it. Get her okay," Bear cautioned. "If you don't she'll kick your scrawny Sicilian ass to the curb. She's scarier on a rampage than any gang."

✦ ✦ ✦

Lily and Bear were sitting on the porch the next morning, cutting coupons out of magazines and newspapers for Jessica's next shopping. "It's Keegan," Lily said looking up when she heard the throaty rumble of the old Chevy Caprice. "Oh! I'm so glad. I was afraid she might have had it with us."

Bear pulled his thumb out of the scissor handle and rubbed it. No scissors were quite big enough for him. "Give up on us? You maybe. But never me."

She would have laughed, but she wasn't sure he was actually joking.

By then, Keegan had left her Caprice and was trudging up the front steps, walking as though her body was outraged with her recent activity. She was dressed in jeans and a sweater that had seen many autumns. Other than a butterfly bandage on one temple and a scratch on the opposite cheek, no wounds were visible.

"Not on duty this weekend?" Bear asked. He turned to Lily and held up a magazine. "Do we need fifty cents off Clearasil?"

"Bear, how many years has it been since any of us had a zit?"

"Just asking." He flipped to another page.

Keegan sat on the bench she usually favored. "Nope. Not on duty. No more duties, not for a while."

"Forced vacation?" Bear asked.

"I'm on official leave. I met with Sheriff Politically Correct Delacruz.

Turns out he didn't even know that I had gone undercover."

"Clay never told him anything?" Bear shook his head while trying to twist his thumb out of the scissor handle once more.

"Not a word. Took me a while to get the boss to believe the whole thing had even happened. I suppose the fact that Officer Galligan is missing is the proof to Delacruz that I'm not completely whacked. The only hard evidence he has are the messages you left on Clay's voice mail. Yes, the boss could access them. And yes, he erased them."

Lily was not surprised. Still she asked, "But what about those awful films?"

Bear asked, "There'll be no investigation, will there?"

Keegan closed her eyes and turned her face to the sun for a long while. Then she looked back at Bear. "A dirty cop like Clay in his department? An asshole like me who never saw it coming? A review of every bust gone wrong for years? No, Delacruz will have no investigation. And, of course, the only other investigative body is the Sapienza family and, oddly enough, they're not talking."

Bear harrumphed. "No, they won't talk. But, Jo, they will do justice at least this one time."

"Justice." She spit out the word like a melon pit. "That leaves it up to me and whether I investigate." Her voice quavered. Lily couldn't tell whether it was anger, sorrow, frustration, hurt. Keegan looked around the ranch for a moment and suddenly stood. "How about giving me a tour? Never have seen all this place. Never rode in Sitting Bull."

"My pleasure," Bear said.

"Give me the scissors and I'll finish here," Lily the Diplomat said. She wanted the two old acquaintances to have the private time they needed. Besides, the cuts made by Bear had such military precision that they made hers look like a child had tried following the coupon borders.

"No, Lily, please come," Keegan said. "You guys are partners, right? No secrets from each other. At least that's how it's supposed to be."

The three trooped through the house and out the back to Sitting Bull. Along the way, Lily and Bear snagged their jackets from a front hall closet.

"You drive, Lily." Bear rarely gave up the controls, but Lily understood his need to concentrate on Keegan. He clambered into the front passenger side leaving the full back seat for her.

They pulled away from the patio, past the horse ring and on toward the barn. Lily knew the point of this tour wasn't really to see the sights so she kept quiet, leaving it up to Bear to talk. After a moment he said, "I called Rita out at the homeless camp first thing this morning. Told her you were okay."

Keegan said, "Thanks for that. She's a good woman. Guess they won't need to worry about that kind of disappearance anymore."

"Count it as a victory, Keegan. And not a small one. Those people have enough issues without kidnapping and murder. You accomplished that. Stopping shit can be more important than investigating it, you know."

Lily slowed the Bull to enter the barn. She'd always found the smell of the horses and the sound of them munching or nickering to be comforting. Keegan might, too. Folly, hearing them from his favorite resting spot in Gina Lola's manger, jumped down and trotted to the Bull. He leaped onto the back seat next to Keegan.

"Off you go, mongrel," Bear said.

"No, Bear." Keegan smiled as Folly gave her a lopsided grin. She scratched behind the floppy ears. "Nothing quite as restorative as a dog."

Bear said, "At least some dogs."

"Tell me about Clay, Bear. I know he's dead, Vinny told me. But tell me about the dogs and how it happened."

Lily turned the Bull around and purred back out of the barn. She passed the pastures where the horses grazed, and putted slowly along the drive where autumn daisies bloomed and wild roses made their last stand for the year. She relived the ugly scene as Bear talked. He minced no words. Keegan deserved to hear it all.

When Bear finished, the deputy asked, "Could you have saved him, Bear?"

That's when Bear chose his words more carefully. "Not much interested in shooting dogs, Keegan. And my aim isn't as good as it used to be."

"Yes. But could you have saved Clay?"

"I don't know if I could. But I know I didn't."

He glanced back at the officer in the back seat. Tears dampened her cheeks although he heard no sound of sobbing. "I had all the proof of evil I needed to make the decision I made."

"But I'm a sworn officer of the law, Bear. I would have killed him myself. And I saw Ghost commit homicide right in front of me. The Ape was no longer a threat when Ghost slit his throat. Said it was for Solana. It was justice. But not the law. Shouldn't I be demanding an investigation? Shouldn't I come forward with all I know regardless of Delacruz? If I'm not upholding the law, who the hell will I become?"

"I'm an old man, Keegan. Here's what I know about life. A guy's got two choices. Turn his back or join in the fray. The law isn't sacrosanct, you know. We change it every day. Vote laws in, vote laws out. But good and evil, well that's a bigger deal. Don't waste time trying to understand the *why* of snuff films and Clay Galligan. Evil just *is*."

Lily finally spoke. "That's what we fight for, people like Bear and me. Charlie and Eunice, too. You can't watch the news without knowing the world is going crazy. The four of us all talked it through again last night. We're committed to it. We'll keep trying to bring a little sanity back to life. Can't be done unless people try."

"As for Ghost," Bear continued, "he's damaged goods, Keegan. He saw the worst when he was too young, too untainted to handle it. Felt betrayed by the human race. You've both been betrayed, but you're not like him. You're tougher, wiser. You'll work this out in time."

Lily had circled back to the front porch and stopped. Keegan got out. "If you two don't mind, I think I might spend a little time around here in the next few days. See if Jessica can teach me to ride one of those beasts."

"It would be wonderful to have you here, Deputy," Lily said with a smile.

"Guess I'll go ask Jessica then. Maybe stop in for a word to Ghost."

"No problem with Jessica," Bear said. "But Ghost is gone. Saw him slip away into the woods first thing this morning. And if Chrissie didn't go drag him back, he's in the wind by now."

CHAPTER THIRTEEN

Case Notes
September 22, 8 p.m.

Sometimes the whole truth does nobody any good. The case of the custom order snuff films is a fine example. Frankie won't tell, the cops won't tell, Solana and Rosie won't tell, we won't tell. But the film makers are out of business nonetheless.

The only one still grappling with the idea of justice is Deputy Josephine Keegan. But she's changing, I think. Sadder but wiser. She has no real heart for arresting the man who saved her. And I really think she'd rather put Clay Galligan's perfidy behind her than dwell on it. I felt exhausted by noon, but the day still had surprises. Eunice has money, you know, and she's an angel to a lot of organizations. One birder group in Alaska has enjoyed her financial support for ages. They've seen their beloved short-tailed albatross edging upward from endangered to merely rare. The group has asked her to come this summer to accept an award.

I knew she wanted to go. But it's a stretch for an octogenarian to get from here to there. Nonetheless, she'd been ordering travel brochures and working on it. I'd gone to our room for forty winks when she pranced in, smiling ear to ear. She announced she'd found a cruise that was in the Alaskan port the very day of the award celebration. She's booked it for us all. We're taking a cruise to Alaska next summer and she's paying for the whole thing!

Maybe we'll go, and maybe we won't. Some or all of us may not make it. That's months from now and anything can happen. But it's fun to think about it. And by then, I'll dance the night away on my new leg! My old one too, of course.

Speaking of dancing. My daughter showed up here just after dinner for her date with Vinny Tononi, and she just set my heart to music. Her beautiful face beamed at him. His looked filled with wonder, as though a queen was smiling in his direction. Damned if he didn't even kiss her hand! I'll bet they'll even ... but that's another story.

- Lily Gilbert, Blessed Assistant to PI Bear Jacobs

THE END

Author's Acknowledgments

For factual content in *Hard to Bear,* I am indebted to many experts, librarians and websites. Any mistakes made are my own.

For critiques that range from sweet to pit bull in temperament, I am sincerely grateful to members of my critique group including Beth Pratt, Bonnie Kuchler and Heidi Hansen. Special thanks, as well, to my 'beta readers' Jan Schamberg, Mindy Mailman, John Overman and Steve Wasilewski whom I trust to tell me when I run off the rails. Without the valued support of Donna Whichello (my researcher, editor, and sister), the gang at Latin's Ranch would not exist. I am also indebted to Vanessa Indelicato, Michael Gribbin and Barry Martin for their unflagging support with social media. To readers of my blog: you are the cheerleaders who keep me going.

Finally, I am indebted to Bear, Lily, Eunice and Charlie who simply refused to disappear after I finished writing *Fun House Chronicles.* That book is the story of how they got together, and the Bear Jacobs Mystery Series tells the tale of their friendship and mission in the days that follow.

About the Author

Linda B. Myers won her first creative contest in the sixth grade for her *Clean Up Fix Up Paint Up* poster. After a Chicago marketing career, she traded in her snow boots for rain boots and moved to the Pacific Northwest with her Maltese Dotty. You can visit with Linda on her blog at www.lindabmyers.com

The Bear Jacobs Mystery Series

Available on www.amazon.com

Meet retired PI Bear Jacobs, his eWatson Lily Gilbert, and the rest of the quirky residents at Latin's Ranch Adult Family Home in the Pacific Northwest. Yes, they are infirm. Yes, they gripe. But all the while, they solve crimes, dodge bullets and stand tall on their canes, walkers and wheels. Enjoy this whole series of cozies with bite.

Book One. **Bear in Mind**

The Latin's Ranch residents investigate the case of Charlie's missing wife. Is she a heart breaking bitch who abandoned her hubby? Or is a madman attacking older women? When others in the community disappear, Bear and his gang follow a dangerous and twisted trail to a surprising conclusion.

Book Two. **Hard to Bear**

A vicious crew is producing old-fashioned snuff films with a violent new twist: custom-order murder for sale. The Latin's Ranch gang takes on the villains behind this updated evil, coming under danger themselves. Bear joins forces with an avenging mob family, a special forces soldier tormented by PTSD, and a pack of mad dogs on the loose in the Pacific Northwest woods.

Novella One. **Bear Claus**

PI Bear Jacobs is mired down with seasonal depression until his e-Watson, Lily, finds him a mystery to solve. The trail is both fun and fearsome as it leads from theft in the My Fair Pair lingerie shop through a local casino to a dangerous solution in the Northwest Forest. Bear Claus is a Christmas novella.

Book Three. **Bear at Sea**

When Eunice wins the Arctic Angel Award, the Latin's Ranch gang cruises to Alaska to pick up her prize. But high life on shipboard is dashed by low life murderers and thieves. One of their aides is struck down, and Eunice's life is threatened not once but twice. The gang takes action, endangering themselves to solve the case of the short-tailed albatross.

Check Out Linda's Other Novels:

Fun House Chronicles

Self-reliant Lily Gilbert enters a nursing home ready to kick administrative butt until the chill realities of the place nearly flatten her. She calls it the Fun House for the scary sights and sounds that await her there. Soon other quirky residents and caregivers draw Lily and her daughter in as they grapple with their own challenges. Lily discovers each stage of life can be its own adventure with more than a few surprises along the way. The characters in the Bear Jacob Mystery series made their first appearance in *Fun House Chronicles*.

Lessons of Evil

Oregon, 1989. Psychologist Laura Covington joins a community mental health department. One of her new clients is so traumatized he suffers Multiple Personality Disorder. Through him, Laura discovers a desert cult and the vicious psychopath who commands it. Laura has unleashed dangerous secrets and now, she must decide how far she is willing to go to protect everything she loves. This is psychological suspense geared to keep you guessing as it builds toward its unpredictable conclusion.

A Time of Secrets: A Big Island Mystery

Life is uncomplicated in a Big Island village until Maile Palea, an 8-year-old girl, disappears. Twelve years later she is still missing. This is the story of her sister and brother who never give up trying to find her and cannot heal until they do, of a village that no longer feels safe from a changing world, and of a perpetrator who discovers what disastrous things happen when you keep secrets too long. A perfect read for fans of edgy suspense and hot Hawaiian nights.

The Slightly Altered History of Cascadia

First Female and Old Man Above have screwed up in the creation of humans and call on the spirit Cascadia to fix it. With the help of her human familiar, a magic blade, a flying bear and a logging horse named Blue, Cascadia takes on a killer, ends the traffic in bear gall bladders, and leads a war against a survivalist group intent on slavery. She devises a plan for a better kind of human. Will the gods agree or scrap the whole damn planet? This satirical adult fantasy is a fast-paced quest through history, mythology and modern day ills.

Excerpt from

BEAR AT SEA

By Linda B. Myers

Book #3 in the Bear Jacobs Mystery Series.

PREFACE

It's quiet now. Eunice and I are both in our beds, needing sleep but it won't happen. Sorrow steals your ability to turn off your brain. I keep playing the whole thing over and over in my head. I cannot conceive of the how and the why. But I'm getting ahead of myself. I need to start before the day went so wrong.

- Lily Gilbert, Assistant to PI Bear Jacobs

INTRODUCTION

The Japanese feather industry damn near plucked the short-tailed albatross population to death. Volcanic eruption at the bird's breeding ground took its toll as well. But WWII really did the trick. Somewhat understandably, the welfare of the albatross was not a top concern at the time. After the war, an American researcher visited Japan's Torishima Island and declared it to be barren of the birds.

But he was wrong.

Juveniles had been growing up while soaring over the Bering Sea during the war years. They flew for months on end, producing a stomach oil that made an energy rich food. Along the way they desalinated their own bodies. When they matured enough to require mates, they returned to the island to breed. Japan and the United States took measures to save them. Today, a fragile population still flies the North Pacific skies.

They were called fool birds by Japanese and boobies by Americans because the albatross is awkward on the ground. They also allow humans to get close enough to kill them. This name-calling might better have been aimed at the people who labeled them. The tail of the short-tailed albatross is no shorter than its relatives, even longer than some. But if they were called long-tailed, then the entity formed to save them would have been called the Protective Association of the Long-Tailed Albatross or PALTA.

And everyone can agree that PASTA is a much catchier acronym.

CHAPTER ONE

Case Notes
May 3, 11 a.m.

Eunice Taylor has always been fond of pasta. But it's not the kind served here at Latin's Ranch Adult Family Care on Sicilian Night that I'm talking about. It's PASTA as in the Protective Association of the Short-Tailed Albatross. Turns out she's a sitting duck for an albatross, so she - and her money - have taken on the PASTA cause big time. Donations, sure. Plus a whopping big endowment for the future.

She surprised everyone but me with an announcement at breakfast one morning not long ago. She held up a photo of a white bird with a blue-tipped pink beak. "This is a short-tailed albatross. These beautiful birds are drowning, caught on hooks or tangled in long-lines dragged by fishing boats." Her false eye lashes fluttered and she patted her silk kaftan in the general area of her heart.

"I'll be damned," muttered Bear Jacobs as he buttered a warm corn muffin. "Could you pass the honey, Lily?"

He could have at least acted like he was interested.

Eunice would not be sidetracked. "It happens to a hundred thousand boobies a year all around the globe." Her orange spiked hair trembled in sympathy with her lower lip.

"Imagine that. A hundred thousand boobies," said Charlie Barker, plopping a dollop of guacamole on his huevos rancheros. "I'd give my eye teeth to see just one nice set again before I die."

"That's not funny, Charlie Barker," Eunice snapped.

"It is not wise for you, this interruption of my little dove," Frankie Sapienza said, staring icicles at Charlie. If the two hadn't been friends, the old capo would have stared something scarier. Like daggers.

"All right, no harm meant," Charlie replied, holding up both hands. "No need to mobilize the mob."

Eunice patted Frankie's hand then resumed. "Through PASTA, I have supported the introduction of by-catch mitigation devices in the North Pacific."

"A by-catch mitigation device. Is that a marital aid?"

"Charlie," growled Bear. "I suggest you let Eunice say her piece and get it over with."

"Thank you, Bear. By-catch mitigation devices are specialized hooks and lines that can save birds or fish that were never meant to be targets. The poor things can disentangle themselves and go free. It's for my efforts on the birds' behalf that I have been awarded PASTA's Arctic Angel Award. I pick it up in a ceremony in Juneau, Alaska on May 18."

Eunice paused for effect. She straightened her back and may have puffed out her chest although the kaftan hid that particular bit of body English. She spread her arms in a graceful movement as though trying to encircle us. "And you're all coming with me!"

Silence while we all looked at Eunice then at each other. Not one of us is on the south side of seventy-five. And not one of us gets around without some help from a fall-on-your-ass mitigation device. Well, except Eunice. Maybe she's forgotten that even though she's an octogenarian, she's spryer than the rest of us.

"Just how do you think we're gonna do that?" asked Bear, who was the only trained investigator in the breakfast room. As his assistant, I keep these case notes. Not that they're real case notes. There isn't a real case, at least not yet. But leave it to a retired private investigator to probe for answers.

"By cruise ship, of course!" Eunice said in the same bright tone she would use to yell 'surprise' at a party. "And I'm paying for the whole thing."

"Juneau?" asked Frankie. He stared at 'his little dove' as though she'd just become his little dingbat.

"Cruise?" asked Bear. His frown deepened the plenty-deep lines in his frowny face.

"Free?" asked Charlie in delight.

"Yes. A cruise ... to Alaska ... and it's free," answered Eunice, nodding from one to the next. "We leave week after next."

"Did you know about this?" Bear swung toward me, his lower jaw jutted out.

"Me? Why would you think I wouldn't tell you about a thing like this?"

Of course, I'd been carrying Eunice's secret while she planned it all out and prepared to deal with the million objections that would follow. I must say I consider Eunice, like the short-tailed albatross, a pretty rare bird. It's hardly her fault that her long association with the bird was soon to lead to 'murder most fowl' for the Latin's Ranch gang.

- Lily Gilbert, Seafaring Assistant to PI Bear Jacobs

Retired PI Bear Jacobs sat at the game table waiting for the others to assemble in the living room for their trip to the senior center. The Latin's Ranch regulars went twice a week to socialize and to give Jessica Winslow, the owner of the adult care home, a little time off from senior sitting. While he waited, Bear was feeding Baby Benny. Baby Benny was seeing just how far he could spit his oatmeal.

"I knew people at the nursing home who acted just like you, champ," Bear muttered. "We're not done 'til you get more of this goop inside than out."

Benny made a facial gesture that Bear chose to interpret as a smile. Jessica had said the baby was sleeping better now and seemed happier more of the time. Bear could feel his iceberg of a heart melt just a bit at the baby's drooly smirk.

"Stay out of the casinos, kid," Bear said. "You got no poker face at all."

Bear was one of Benny's favorites. The old man could have been mistaken for a stuffed version of his namesake. His head was round, his eyes dark as black beads, his brown beard and hair shot through with gray. His arms were a genuine bear hug that held the baby safe from a dangerous world. They often sat together when Jessica needed a helping hand.

Nobody spoke of it, as though talk could make it real. No need to court disaster. But Bear knew all the residents hoped for the same thing: that this baby would rise above the crack and booze that may have poisoned his system in the womb. Their caregiver Jessica was Benny's mother now. She and Ben Stassen had adopted him after Ben's daughter disappeared back onto the Seattle streets, leaving her baby behind.

Bear was making yummy noises that Baby Benny was ignoring when the big man heard the sound of Lily's cane tapping the floor. "Just look at these beauties," she said as she walked into the room holding a vase bursting with reds, yellows and whites. The strong aroma of species roses wafted into the living room with her. Bear knew she loved to be out on the patio, working with their container garden. He figured a fresh breeze was responsible for the pink in her cheeks and her disorganized cloud of white hair.

Charlie looked up from the sports page and smiled. "Still a pleasure to see you walk into a room, Lily. It's a sight to behold."

"One of these days, Charlie, I may even skip like a little girl." Lily had received her new prosthetic leg at the start of the year. She'd pushed through pain and fear of falling and threats of deadly infection that could manifest where the artificial and the real leg joined. At facing down problems with dogged determination, Lily was a rock star. Her wheelchair was a thing of the past, and she only used her rolling walker at times when she removed the prosthesis. Otherwise, she employed a cane to help her with balance. Her physical therapist said she'd always feel more secure with one. Then he'd shrugged and added, "Of course, I'm thinking of normal people."

Eunice came into the room just after Lily, a sprig of clematis tucked over an ear. Rhinestones in her sunglass frames twinkled and little bells in her earrings tinkled. "It's gorgeous outside. And so warm I only need a shawl." She was wrapped in an eye-popping red and black scarf with the Salish tribal art pattern of hummingbirds. "Every blooming thing is having a field day. Even the horses are racing around the pasture feeling their oats."

"Eunice," Bear said, interrupting her song of spring in a far less lyrical voice.

She stopped. In fact, his tone was serious enough that they all looked up. "Yes, Bear?"

"About this cruise."

She bloomed again. "Doesn't it sound fun? I have brochures we can share at the senior center today." She patted the tote bag she carried, the one she'd Bedazzled with *GOOD VIBES.*

"Guess I don't need to wait 'til then to tell you." He wanted to get this over with.

"Tell me what, Bear?" Eunice took a seat next to him at the game table, looking like a worried ginger poodle. Baby Benny made a grab for her tote, a fat little fist wrapping around the blingy strap.

"I'm not going."

"What?" said Charlie, Lily and Eunice, pretty much in unison.

"It's very generous of you, Eunice, but it's not for me. Cruising."

"Why not?"

"Spent time in troop carriers in Nam, you know. Never much liked boats ever since."

"Oh! But this isn't a boat ride, Bear. This is a luxury *ship.* Taking people to beautiful places."

"Never much liked people, either, come to think of it."

"All your friends will be there," Eunice said, once again holding her arms wide to include everyone in the room. "You won't have to talk to strangers if you don't want to."

"Well, I don't want to, and there's almost no chance of it if I stay here."

"Some of them strangers might be real lookers," Charlie cut in. "I know you got an eye for a redhead when you see one."

Bear began to feel cornered. And that meant he could get dangerous. "Not that it's any of your business, people, but I get seasick. There. That's the end of it." He shut his mouth tight, not unlike Baby Benny when faced with a spoonful of medicine.

At that moment, Jessica breezed in and picked up the baby. "Thanks for watching him, Bear." She wrinkled her nose. "Hmmm. Smells like he needs a change."

"Yep. Goop to poop in next to no time."

"I'll see to it. Vinny's out front waiting for you all." The Cadillac could handle all five residents. "Frankie's already in the car."

"We'll talk more about it at the senior center," said Lily.

"Nothin' more to talk about. I'm not going." Bear stood, waited a couple seconds for his hips to stop barking, and *kachunked* on his quad cane out of the room. But he wasn't so far ahead that he didn't overhear the rest of them as he went out the door.

A crestfallen Eunice said, "He must know he can wear a patch for seasickness. Just behind his ear."

"It must be serious," said Charlie, unlocking the wheels of his chair and following the rest of the pack. "Redheads can usually bring him around."

✦ ✦ ✦

After a few hours of entertainment at the senior center, Vinny Tononi drove the group back home to Latin's Ranch. The Cadillac was approximately the same size as a cruise ship. Frankie, Eunice and Charlie sat in the back. Lily was sandwiched up front between Bear and Vinny.

Vinny was Frankie's bodyguard, chauffer and all around *goomba*. He was big, stern and often clanked with concealed weaponry. There was a time when he made Lily nervous. Now that he was her daughter's *amore*, Lily was edgier than ever. The high probability that one of them would end up broken hearted - or *cuore spezzato* depending - made her as jumpy as a jackrabbit.

Vinny took his eyes from the road long enough to look down at Lily. "You are well, Miss Lily? You are so quiet."

"Oh fine, fine. Just enjoying the spring color." Rhodies flashed by pink white pink white pink white as the vehicle zoomed toward home.

In fact, she wasn't fine. Their visit to the senior center had been unsatisfactory. First, she'd lost to a newcomer at Scrabble. That simply wouldn't do, and she needed a rematch soon. Then she'd made an effort to talk with Bear while he and Frankie checked and checkmated each other. But the big man wasn't talking about the cruise. She'd have to wait for a moment alone with him to find out the skinny.

Seasick?

That was bullshit and she just knew it.

They were approaching the Latin's Ranch driveway when Bear's phone rang. He frisked himself before locating the little device in a shirt pocket.

"What?" he asked into it when he found it. "No, we're gone ... no, I didn't ... no ... yeah. I think you maybe should stop by."

Bear clicked off. Lily watched him cloud over like a front moving in. She waited. Finally, she couldn't take it anymore. "Who was that? What's happened?"

"Someone was shot at the senior center right after we left. Cupcake's coming to talk about it." He turned his great head toward the back seat. "Eunice?"

"Bear?"

"Think I might go to Alaska with you after all."

CHAPTER TWO

Case Notes
May 3, 9 p.m.

Deputy Detective Josephine Keegan of the Major Crimes Unit stopped by at about six o'clock. Jo is a special favorite of all the Latin's Ranch gang ever since we worked that missing person case together. She's pretty good at telling us whether we're being helpful or buttinskies without hurting our feelings. It's a gift.

Bear knew her as a rookie sheriff's deputy long before he hung up his holster as a private investigator. He calls her Cupcake from back in the day. She hates it now, and I imagine she hated it then. But it's hard for an old Bear to change his stripes especially if he doesn't want to. Jo is a handsome woman but maybe a little less so than she used to be. After the painful fiasco with her partner Clay, she's become a sadder but wiser cupcake. You can see it in the set of her jaw and the wispy lines beginning to show around her eyes. More defensive, less likely to smile. Her dark hair is pulled straight back in a tight knot without one strand daring to misbehave. And I have to say, she's overly tough on her partners now. Snappish. I imagine the boys in the department call her a bitch. No. I imagine they call her worse than that.

I think she's on partner number three since Clay. This one must be scared of her. At least when she told him to stay outside, he nodded, muttered "Ma'am," and stayed. He sat on the porch while Furball explored the overall suitability of his lap for a cat nap. That cat lays claim to all comfort zones before Jessica's dog, Folly, even has a chance.

Bear pissed me off when he said he'd see Jo alone, meaning without me, his eWatson. How the hell can I keep the case notes if he keeps the case to himself? So I decided while the big man got the story from Jo, I'd take a run at the partner.

I started my investigation with a plate of our cook Aurora's biscochitos. Even a hard-boiled cop would spill his guts for a couple of those cinnamon sugar cookies. And this guy was so far from hard-boiled he'd be child's play to crack.

- Lily Gilbert, Investigative Assistant to PI Bear Jacobs

Lily put on her sweet face and approached the target. "Hello, young man. My name is Lily Gilbert. I thought you might like a bit of refreshment while you wait out here." She set the plate of cookies on the little wicker occasional table beside his chair. Then she sat on the glider next to it and smiled broadly at the plump twenty-something officer.

He touched his hat brim. "Ma'am," he said.

Lily wondered if *ma'am* was the only word he knew. It was the only one she'd heard him say to Jo Keegan. Maybe he was merely shy. "And who might you be, young man?" she prompted.

"Deputy Detective Brandon Orwell at your service." He made a move to stand politely, but Furball hissed and extended a fistful of threatening claws in the direction of his crotch. Detective Orwell sat back down with extreme haste.

Lily decided he might be shy but he wasn't stupid. As he kept an eye on the fat orange cat, she said, "I'm the assistant to the private investigator that your partner is here to consult."

"A PI lives here?" He looked around quizzically at the farm house, the pastures, the barn. Nothing could look more bucolic. "My partner wants to consult with a PI?"

"Yes to both your questions."

He pursed his lips just a bit. Lily assumed he was grappling with Law Officer Conviction Number One, that official detectives never consult unofficial detectives.

"I know it is rare. But you see, this one was her mentor. Taught her everything she knows."

"Really? She knows a lot."

Clearly he believed Jo was not merely a ball buster but a knowledgeable one.

"Take a cookie, my dear. Enjoy while you have a brief break from your important duties. Now then, my friend Jo had a few things she wanted me to ask you while she talks to PI Jacobs."

"She did?" He took a bite of heaven and began to melt. "Wow, that's good."

"Have another." Pushing drugs couldn't be easier. "She asked that you give me your overall impression of what happened. You know, your take. Important to have an expert opinion before it is contaminated by others."

"Really? She called mine an expert opinion?" He actually beamed.

"Something very much like that. The exact words escape me. My memory isn't what it used to be, you see. But I am sure that was the sense of it. So, what time did the incident occur?"

"Well it must have happened between three and four pm, although forensics will have to confirm."

"Just tell me in your own words."

"An old lady bought it. Er, I mean a senior citizen was found deceased."

Now that he was talking, Lily had no intention of letting him stop. "Inside the senior center?"

"In their parking lot. Between two parked cars."

"How did she die?"

"Strangled is how it looked to me."

"Strangled?" Lily was surprised. Of course, no bullet meant no sound. "Did she scream? What was the weapon? A rope? A wire? Approached from behind? In front?"

"Behind. Strangled with a scarf. Nobody has reported hearing anything but we've just begun to interview -"

"A scarf? One of her own?"

Hadn't it been too warm for a scarf? Well except for the one that …

"Yes, ma'am. A big square one. People saw her with it over her shoulders earlier in the day."

"A thin scarf like silk? Or heavy like wool?" In Lily's stomach butterflies were upping the game from flutter to thrash.

"Thin, ma'am. Bright red with a -"

The front door swung open. Detective Keegan came out, followed by Bear. Keegan barked, "Brandon!"

This time, the young man leaped up spilling Furball to the ground. The cat left a long scratch on his arm as it landed on its feet, lifted its tail and swayed away.

"Brandon, have you been yapping to this sweet little lady?"

"She said -"

"You've been played, kid. By an old woman with more curiosity than that cat. The scratch serves you right."

Lily continued playing the hostess. "I'll get a couple bandages, young man." Turning to the detective she said, "Care for some sugar cookies, Jo?"

"Thanks but no thanks, Miss Lily. Things are syrupy enough around here as is. And I have bandages in the cruiser. We'll just be on our way."

"Well, okay then, officers. Nice to meet you, Brandon."

He touched his hat once again. "Ma'am."

Bear *kachunked* on his cane over to the glider and sat next to Lily. As they watched the deputies depart in their cruiser, he hummed *Let's Go On a Sentimental Journey.*

Lily knew that he hummed when he was thinking. When the cruiser's dust in the drive had settled, he said to her, "You're worried."

She didn't answer.

"And you're pissed at me."

"Yes. Worried and pissed in equal measure."

"That's why I wanted to talk to Cupcake alone. No reason to worry you if this had nothing to do with Eunice. It would have worked if it weren't for Officer Spill The Beans." "So you knew about the red scarf?" She gave some thought to being mad at him for withholding information, but decided she'd rather listen than argue. At least this one time.

"When Jo called me, she mentioned it. And I saw the woman wearing it earlier myself. The scarf looked a lot like the one Eunice had on. Bright red with a pattern. Not birds maybe, but easy to confuse from a distance if the perp didn't know the victim personally."

"You think some stranger meant to kill Eunice?"

"Don't know. Probably not. My guess is a random attack. But it's not a bad time to sail away. Get her out of the area."

Lily knew Bear wasn't crazy about admitting he might be worried, too. But his next statement was a confession to just that. "Get you away, too, since you'd protect her. If she's in danger, you're in danger."

Lily drew a breath, held and expelled it. "It can't be about Eunice. Who the hell would want to hurt her other than the fashion police?"

"Nobody. Probably."

"I don't want to scare her, Bear. She's having such fun planning this trip."

"Then we won't tell her our suspicions. Just keep our eyes open until we're underway. I meant it when I said I'm going, too."

"Probably shouldn't tell Frankie either or the mob will overrun the ranch."

Bear snorted in agreement. "Last time that happened, Jessica used some damn colorful words for me."

They sat and glided for a while in companionable silence listening to the squeak of the metal accompany the song of a Western tanager. Then he added, "Keegan may have to talk with Eunice, but she'll be discreet. Or leave it up to me."

"You? Discreet?"

Lily could tell he was gathering steam to lecture her about his level of prudence vs hers when the front door opened again. Their youngest aide, Alita Aarons, leaned out and chirped, "There you are! Time for dinner you two. From the aroma of the *arroz con pollo*, I'd say Aurora has outdone herself again."

✦ ✦ ✦

It was a full house for dinner with all five residents, Vinny, Sam Hart the barn manager, Jessica, Ben and Baby Benny. Aurora and Alita served the *arroz con pollo* along with an avocado salad and crusty rolls. Many appreciative noises were made, but the death of the unknown woman was the real buzz.

"You go to a place as safe as a senior center and what happens? A murder, that's what!" Jessica shook her head causing her curls to dance. She looked up at the man who had been her husband for less than three months and rolled her beautiful blue eyes dramatically. "I can't turn my back on them, not for a minute."

Bennett Stassen was not only Jessica's new husband but the baby's natural grandfather as well as adoptive father. Everyone at the table knew he was consumed with doing all jobs well. At the moment he was engaged in another skirmish with Baby Benny regarding food intake. This one was over mashed carrots. By the looks of the highchair, floor and Ben's shirt, Baby Benny was winning. Grandpa Dad said, "Can't talk now, Jess. I'll get the hang of this if I concentrate."

"Besides, it wasn't one of us, Jess," Charlie said regarding the senior center murder. "We're all okay. So what's the worry?"

"Who was it, Bear? The deceased?" Jessica asked.

The group turned toward him. "Don't know. Hadn't seen her before today. According to Cupcake, her I.D. says she's from Idaho. Apparently visiting friends in the area."

He helped himself to a second serving of chicken as Eunice asked, "Why did Detective Keegan come talk to you?"

"Oh, just because we go to the senior center so often. You know, familiar with the scene of the crime and all. Might give her a few helpful hints." It didn't sound very believable even to Bear, but Lily helped him out by changing the subject.

"What will you be doing while we're on the cruise, Jessica?"

"We'll be on vacation here, of course, without you guys around to pester us. Sleep late, sit around and relax, romantic dinners ..."

Baby Benny had had enough and wailed like a fire siren. Ben got up to clean him up.

"Use the horse trough in the pasture. Big enough to dunk yourself, too," Sam called after him.

"You better send the kid with us if you hope for peace and quiet," Bear said to Jessica. "He'd fit in my duffle."

"Don't tempt me. Now then. I have all your birth certificates in a file for you." As the owner of Latin's Ranch, Jessica held most of their records. "Good idea to take a passport if you have one. If not, since the ship goes and comes from the same port, your driver's license should be okay."

Bear smiled to himself as Jessica tried to appear stern. Her curls, freckles and big blue eyes weren't the stuff of strictness. "But I don't want any of you driving, is that clear? In fact, nothing dangerous. Promise?"

"Except maybe that helicopter excursion over the fjords," said Bear.

"The dog sleds on Mendenhall Glacier," said Eunice.

"The zip line in Icy Point," said Frankie although in a Sicilian accent it sounded more like zeep line.

"The trek through grizzly country," said Lily.

"Shooting in a small boat the rapids," said Vinnie also accent-challenged.

"A shipboard romance," said Charlie while playing the air violin.

Jessica held up her hands like a traffic cop. "Knock it off all of you, or I won't take you to the dock on departure day."

By the time Aurora served coffee spiked with cinnamon and clove -- along with a dollop of vanilla ice cream or shot of tequila for those who wanted it -- the conversation had devolved to the subject of packing. Bear figured his duffle would work for him. But Eunice was going to need at least three mega-bags. And they had a small herd of mobility equipment from wheelchairs to canes.

The only device they'd leave behind was Sitting Bull, their customized golf cart. So they better have no need for quick escapes. Of course, why would they need something like that on a luxury cruise?

END OF EXCERPT

Visit with Linda B. Myers at

www.LindaBMyers.com
facebook.com/lindabmyers.author
myerslindab@gmail.com
amazon.com/author/lindabmyers